Hole
in the
Middle

Hole
in the
Middle

Coco Simon

Simon Spotlight

New York London Toronto Sydney New Delhi

An imprint of Simon & Schuster Children's Publishing Division
1230 Avenue of the Americas, New York, New York 10020
This Simon Spotlight hardcover edition December 2019
Copyright © 2019 by Simon & Schuster, Inc.
All rights reserved, including the right of reproduction in whole or in part in any form.
SIMON SPOTLIGHT and colophon are registered trademarks of Simon & Schuster, Inc.
Text by Valerie Dobrow
For information about special discounts for bulk purchases, please contact Simon & Schuster Special Sales at 1-866-506-1949 or business@simonandschuster.com.
Designed by Ciara Gay
The text of this book was set in Bembo Std.
Manufactured in the United States of America 1019 FFG
10 9 8 7 6 5 4 3 2 1
ISBN 978-1-5344-6026-3 (hc)
ISBN 978-1-5344-6025-6 (pbk)
ISBN 978-1-5344-6027-0 (eBook)
Library of Congress Catalog Card Number 2019946650

Chapter One
Donuts Are My Life

My grandmother started Donut Dreams, a little counter in my family's restaurant that sells her now-famous homemade donuts, when my dad was about my age. The name was inspired by my grandmother's dream to save enough money from the business to send him to any college he wanted, even if it was far away from our small town.

It worked. Well, it kind of worked. I mean, my grandmother's donuts are pretty legendary. Her counter is so successful that instead of only selling donuts in the morning, the shop is now open all day. Her donuts have even won all sorts of awards, and there are rumors that there's a cooking show on TV that might come film a segment about how she started Donut Dreams from virtually nothing.

My grandmother, whom I call Nans—short for Nana—raised enough money to send my dad to college out of state all the way in Chicago. But then he came back. I've heard Nans was happy about that, but I'm not because it means I'm stuck here in this small town.

So now it's my turn to come up with my own "donut dreams," because I am dreaming about going to college in a big, glamorous city somewhere far, far away. Dad jokes that if I do go to Chicago, I have to come back like he did.

No way, I thought to myself. Nobody ever moves here, and nobody ever seems to move away, either. It's just the same old, same old, every year: the Fall Fling, the Halloween Hoot Fair, Thanksgiving, Snowflake Festival, New Year's, Valentine's Day and the Sweetheart Ball . . . I mean, we know what's coming.

Everyone makes a big deal about the first day of school, but it's not like you're with new kids or anything. There's one elementary school, one middle school, and one high school.

Our grandparents used to go to a regional school,

which meant they were with kids from other towns in high school. But the school was about forty-five minutes away, and getting there and back was a big pain, so they eventually decided to keep everyone at the high school here. It's a big old building where my dad went to school, and his brother and my aunt, and just about everyone else's parents.

Some kids do go away for college. My BFF Casey's sister, Gabby, is one of them. She keeps telling Casey that she should go to the same college so they can live together while Gabby goes to medical school, which is her dream. It's a cool idea, but what's the point of moving away from everything if you just end up moving in with your sister?

Maybe it's that I don't have a sister, I have a brother, and living with him is messy. I mean that literally. Skylar is ten. He spits globs of toothpaste in the sink, his clothes are all over his room, and he drinks milk directly from the carton, which makes Nans shriek.

My grandparents basically live with us now, which is a whole long story. Well, the short story is that my mother died two years ago. After Mom died, everyone was a mess, so Nans and Grandpa ended up helping out a lot. Their house is only a short drive

3

down the street from us, so it makes sense they're around all the time.

Even their dog comes over now, which is good because I love him, but weird because Mom would never let us get a pet. I still feel like she's going to come walking in the door one day and be really mad that there's a dog running around with muddy paws.

My mother was an artist. She was an art teacher in the middle school where I'm starting this year, which will be kind of weird.

There's a big mural that all her students painted on one wall of the school after she died. The last time I was in the school was when they had a ceremony and put a plaque next to it with her name on it. Now I'll see it every day.

It's not like I don't think about her every day anyway. Her studio is still set up downstairs. It's a small room off the kitchen with great light. For a while none of us went in there, or we'd just kind of tiptoe in and see if we could still smell her.

Lately we use it more. I like to go in and sit in her favorite chair and read. It's a cozy chair with lots of pillows you can kind of sink into, and I like to think it's her giving me a hug. Dad uses her big worktable to do paperwork. The only people who don't go in are Nans and Grandpa. Dad grumbles that it's the one room in the house that Nans hasn't invaded.

Sometimes I catch Nans in the doorway, though, just looking at Mom's paintings on the walls. Mom liked to paint pictures of us and flowers. One wall is covered in black-and-white sketches of us and the other is this really cool, colorful collection of painted flowers with some close up, some far away, and some in vases. I could stare at them for hours.

I remember there used to be fresh flowers all over the house. Mom even had little vases with flowers in the bathrooms, which was a little crazy, especially since Skylar always knocked them over and there would be puddles of water everywhere.

Sometimes when I had a bad day she'd make a special little arrangement for me and put it next to my bed. When she was sick, I used to go out to her garden and cut them and make little bouquets for her. I'd put them on her night table, just like she did for me. Nans always makes sure there are flowers on the kitchen table, but it's not really the same.

Grandpa and Nans own a restaurant called the Park View Table. Locals call it the Park for short.

They don't get any points for originality, because the restaurant is literally across from a park, so it has a park view. But it seems to be the place in town where everyone ends up.

On the weekends everyone stops by in the mornings, either to pick up donuts and coffee or for these giant pancakes that everyone loves. Lunch is busy during the week, with everyone on their lunch breaks and some older people who meet there regularly, and dinnertime is the slowest. I know all this because I basically grew up there.

Nans comes up with the menus and the specials, and she's always trying out new recipes with the chef. Or on us. Luckily, Nans is a great cook, but some of her "creative" dishes are a little too kooky to eat.

Nans still makes a lot of the donuts, but Dad does too, especially the creative ones. Donut Dreams used to have just the usual sugar or jelly-filled or chocolate, which were all delicious, but Dad started making PB&J donuts and banana crème donuts.

At first people laughed, but then they started to try them. Word of mouth made the donuts popular, and for a little while, people were confused because they didn't realize Donut Dreams was a counter inside the Park. They instead kept looking for a donut shop.

My uncle Charlie gives my dad a hard time sometimes, teasing him that he's the "big-city boy with the fancy ideas." Uncle Charlie loves my dad, and my dad loves him, but I sometimes wonder if Uncle Charlie and Aunt Melissa are a little mad that Dad got to go away to school and they went to the state school nearby.

My dad runs Donut Dreams. Uncle Charlie does all the ordering for food and napkins and everything you need in a restaurant, and Aunt Melissa is the accountant who manages all the financial stuff, like the payroll and paying all the bills. So between my dad, his brother, and his sister, and the cousins working at the restaurant, it's a lot of family, all the time.

My brother, Skylar, and I are the youngest of seven cousins. I like having cousins, but some of them think they can tell me what to do, and that's five extra people bossing me around.

"There's room for everyone in the Park!" Grandpa likes to say when he sees us all running around, but honestly, sometimes the Park feels pretty crowded.

That's the thing: in a small town, I always feel like there are too many people. Maybe it's just that there are too many people I know, or who know me.

Right after Mom died I couldn't go anywhere without someone coming up to me and putting an arm around me or patting me on the head. People were nice, don't get me wrong, but everyone knows everything in a small town. Sometimes I feel like I can't breathe.

Mom grew up outside of Chicago, and that's where my other grandmother, her mother, still lives. I call her Mimi. We go there every Thanksgiving, which I love. I remember asking her once when we were at the supermarket why there were so many people she didn't know. She laughed and explained that she lived in a big town, where most people don't know each other.

It fascinated me that she could walk into the supermarket and no one there would know where she had just been, or that she bought a store-bought cake and was going to tell everyone she baked it. No one was peering into her cart and asking what she was making for lunch, or how the tomatoes tasted last week. Nans always wonders if Mimi is lonely, since she lives by herself, but it sounds nice to me.

Everyone in our family pitches in, but I officially

start working at Donut Dreams next week for a full shift every day, which is kind of nice. I'll work for Dad. He bought me a T-shirt that says THE DREAM TEAM that I can wear when I'm behind the counter.

We have a couple of really small tables near the counter that are separate from the restaurant, so people can sit down and eat their donuts or have coffee. I'll have to clean those and make sure that the floor around them is swept too.

Uncle Charlie computerized the ordering systems last year, so all I'll have to do is just swipe what someone orders and it'll total it for me, keep track of the inventory, and even tell me how much change to give, which is good because Grandpa is a real stickler about that.

"A hundred pennies add up to a dollar!" he always yells when he finds random pennies on the floor or left on a table.

Dad will help me set up what we're calling my "Dream Account," which is a bank account where I'll deposit my paycheck. I figure if I can save really well for six years, I can have a good portion to put toward my dream college.

So we're going to the bank. And of course my

friend Lucy's mom works there. Because you can't go anywhere in this town without knowing someone.

"Well, hi, honey," she said. "Are you getting your own savings account? I'll bet you're saving all that summer money for new clothes!"

"Nope," said Dad. "This is college money."

"Oh, I see," she said, smiling. "In that case, let's make this official." She started typing information into the computer. "Okay. I have your address because I know it. . . ." She tapped the keyboard some more.

See what I mean? Everyone knows who I am and where I live. I wonder if people at the bank know how much money we have too.

After a few minutes, it was all set up. Afterward Dad showed me how to make a deposit and gave me my own bank card too.

I was so excited, not only because I had my own bank account, which felt very grown-up, but because the Dream Account was now crossed off my list, which meant I was that much closer to making my dream come true. I was almost hopping up and down in my seat in the car.

"You really want to get out of here, don't you?" asked Dad, and when he said it, it wasn't in his usual joking way. He sounded a little worried, and I immediately felt bad. It wasn't as if I just wanted to get away from Dad.

"You know," he said thoughtfully, "I get it."

"You do?" I asked.

"Yeah," he said. "I was the same way. I was itchy. I wanted to go see the big wide world."

We both stared ahead of us.

"I don't want to go to get away from you and Skylar," I said.

Dad nodded.

"But think of Wetsy Betsy."

Dad looked confused. "Who is Wetsy Betsy?"

"Wetsy Betsy is Elizabeth Ellis. In kindergarten she had an accident and wet her pants. And even now, like, seven years later, kids still call her Wetsy Betsy. It's like once you're known as something here, you can't shake it. You can't . . ." I trailed off.

"You can't reinvent yourself, you mean?" asked Dad.

"Exactly!" I said. "You are who you are and you can't ever change." I could tell Dad's mind was spinning.

"So who are you?" he asked after a few more minutes.

"What?" I asked.

"Who are you?" Dad asked. "If Elizabeth Ellis is Wetsy Betsy, then who are you?"

I took a deep breath. "I'm the girl whose mother died. I sometimes hear kids whisper about it when I walk by."

I saw Dad grimace. I looked out the window so I wouldn't have to watch him. We stayed quiet the rest of the way home.

We pulled up into our driveway and Dad turned off the car, but he didn't get out.

"I understand, honey. I really do. I understand dreaming. I understand getting away, starting fresh, starting over. But wherever you go, you take yourself with you, just remember that. You can start a new chapter and change things around, but sometimes you can't just rewrite the entire book," he said.

I thought about that. I didn't quite believe what he was saying, though. In school they were always nagging us about rewriting things.

"But you escaped," I said. "And then you just came back!"

"Well, you escape prison. I didn't see this place as a prison," Dad said. "But Nans as a warden, that's . . ."

He started laughing. "Seriously, though, I left because I wanted an adventure. I wanted to meet new people and see if I could make it in a place where everyone didn't care about me and where I was truly on my own. I never had any plans to come back, but that's how it worked out."

"So why did you move back here?" I asked.

"Because of Mom," said Dad. "She loved this place. I brought her here to meet everyone and she didn't want to leave."

"But Mimi didn't want her to move here," I said, trying to piece together what happened.

I had always thought it was Dad who wanted to move back home. Mom and Dad met in college. She lived at school like Dad did, but Mimi was close by, so she could drive over for dinner. Mom and Dad hung out at Mimi's house a lot while they were in college.

"Noooo," Dad said slowly. "Mimi wasn't too thrilled about Mom's plan. She didn't really understand why Mom would want to move out here, so far from her family, and especially where there weren't a lot of opportunities for artists."

"So she changed her mind?" I asked.

I never remembered Mimi saying anything bad

about where we lived, but Dad would always tease her, saying, "So it worked out okay, didn't it, Marla?"

She came to visit twice a year and always seemed to have a good time. "It's a beautiful place to live," she would say, smiling.

"Well," said Dad. "It took Mimi a while to change her mind. But she saw how happy Mom was and how much everyone here loved Mom, so she was happy that Mom was happy. That's the thing about parents. They really just want their kids to be happy, even if they don't understand why they do things. If you decide to move away from here, I'll miss you every day, but if that's what you want to do and that's what makes you happy, then I will be there with the moving truck."

"So if I tell you I want to move to Chicago for college, you'll be okay with that?" I asked.

"If you promise to come home and visit me a lot," said Dad, grinning.

"Deal!" I said.

"I love you," said Dad.

"I love you back," I said.

"Okay, kiddo, let's go in for dinner. Nans goes mad when we're late."

"Dad, isn't it correct to say that Nans gets angry? Because, like, animals go mad but people get angry."

"In that definition, Lindsay, I think that is an entirely correct way to categorize your grandmother when you are late for dinner. She gets mad!"

I giggled and opened the car door.

"Ready, set, run to the warden!" said Dad, and we raced up to the house, bursting with laughter.

Chapter Two
First Day of Work

The plan was that I'd start working at Donut Dreams two weeks before school started. That way I'd get into my regular routine and not have to adjust to a job at the Park and a new school at the same time. For the school year, I'll work after school two days a week and one day on the weekends.

But since much of the waitstaff take vacations at the end of the summer, it was all hands on deck, according to Grandpa, and the whole family was taking full-day shifts at the restaurant.

Mornings were always way complicated because things start early in the restaurant business. Even if the Park didn't open until six thirty in the morning, that meant everyone, including the cooks, the busboys, and the waitresses, got there by five o'clock to start prepping the food, brewing coffee, sorting the daily bread deliveries, and making sure the ovens were on.

Since we own Donut Dreams, everyone just assumes that we eat donuts at every meal, and that they're stacked everywhere in our house. But we actually eat like everyone else, and Nans only lets us have donuts on the weekends, just like Mom did.

So Monday morning I put on my Dream Team T-shirt and got downstairs early. Nans already had my fruit and juice at my place at the table. Since she got up early to make the donuts, by the time Skylar and I got up, she joked that she should be making lunch. Dad had to be at the restaurant early in the morning, so after Mom died, Nans was the one who came back home from the restaurant to stay with us when Dad had to leave.

Nans was making me scrambled eggs and I was surprised to see Skylar, still in his pj's, eating his cereal.

"What are you doing up?" I asked. "It's not like you have to go to work today."

"Nans woke me up," he whined. "We have to drive you to work. So even if I don't have to go to work, I still have to get up."

"You can get in the car in your pajamas!" Nans said, exasperated. "I just can't leave you here alone while I run Lindsay to work!"

Skylar rolled his eyes. "Well, can I at least get a donut while we're there?"

Nans sighed. "Sure," she said with a grin. "On Saturday."

It probably seems weird to eat breakfast before you go to work in a restaurant, but working in a restaurant is hard, and you don't get a lot of breaks. It's not like you can stuff snacks in your apron pockets either. You're on your feet the whole time and running around, and you can barely sip a drink, let alone eat. During slow times the staff will grab a plate in the kitchen, but as soon as you have a customer you have to put it down, so no one ever has a leisurely burger or anything.

Nans jingled her keys, and Skylar sighed loudly and pushed back his chair. I took one last look in the mirror before we left, and then Nans drove down the curvy road toward the restaurant.

I could ride my bike to work, especially in nice weather, but Mom would never, ever let us ride on Park Street. She said people went too fast around the curves.

It's kind of weird that even though Mom died, some of her rules are still here, and nobody has tried to get rid of them. At first we did things like staying up really late because everyone was so distracted, and nobody seemed to notice. Plus, there were, like, hundreds of people at the house and stopping in at all hours.

But one night at dinner, Dad said, "Okay, life as we know it is going to be very different, but there are ground rules that stay the same."

After that we had bedtimes and regular meals and all the old rules seemed to kick back in.

When we pulled up to the restaurant, it was six fifteen. You could tell Nans was torn, because she wanted to go in and check things out and get a few things done in the office, but Sky was scowling.

Nans glanced in the back seat. "Sky, do you want to go say hi to your dad?"

But before he could answer, Dad came bounding out of the restaurant. "A fine family morning!" he bellowed, smiling at me. "Look at this wonderful employee on her first day at Donut Dreams!"

He actually looked really proud, and I kind of blushed a little.

"She's going to be spectacular, as always!" said Nans, smiling.

"And I get to see my boy!" said Dad, reaching in to give Sky a squeeze.

"I had to get up early," Skylar whined.

"Good practice for when school starts!" said Dad. "And since you made the very big effort of getting into the car, I have a little treat for you." He handed Skylar a bag.

"Donuts!" screamed Skylar, and Dad laughed.

"First-day-of-work exception," Dad said. "Don't get too used to it!" He gave Skylar a kiss on the head and added, "Have fun at camp!"

Then he turned to me and opened the car door. "And you, my dear, are mine for the day. Let's get to work!"

My cousin Kelsey was also working behind the counter at Dreams, and she gave me a quick wave when I came in.

Kelsey and my other four cousins all work at the Park and Dreams. Kelsey is only older than me by a month and a half, but she always tells people I'm her younger cousin.

"You know what to do?" asked Kelsey.

I nodded and slipped behind the counter with her and put on an apron. Dad was talking to the manager of the restaurant about something, so I turned around and stared at the rows of donuts, making sure they were all lined up and that the shelves were clean.

When Mom was alive I went home right after school, but after she died, Dad would pick Skylar and me up and bring us to the restaurant so we could be near him. We'd hang out at a table and do our homework or color for a few hours before Nans would take us home for dinner. I had watched the counter at Dreams for a few years, so now I knew exactly what had to be done.

If you look around, a restaurant is kind of a fascinating place. It's usually busy—if it's a good restaurant, that is—and there are people sitting and talking about stuff, and if you pay attention, you can learn a lot. And most people don't stop talking when someone comes over to the table. So even if I helped clear a table or dropped off a glass of water, I could really get an earful. That's what I loved most, picking up little pieces about people that you wouldn't normally know.

Grandpa loves to go around and talk to everyone,

and he stops and chats with the regulars, especially the ones at the counter in the morning. He knows everything that was going on in town, but he never spilles it to any of us, which drove Mom crazy.

"Oh, come on," she'd say. "I know they were probably talking about it at the Park. What's the dirt?"

And he would just smile and shake his head and say, "I just pour the coffee. What do I know?"

But Grandpa never misses a beat, so you have to be on your toes. I once saw him correct people for not properly wiping down a table, or not setting it right, or sloshing a glass of water when they put it down.

I know that he likes things tidy, which is hard when you sell donuts, because some of them have sprinkles or are crumbly. So when you lift them off the tray, you get crumbs everywhere—on the shelf, on the floor, and sometimes on the counter.

At Dreams there's a lot of wiping and sweeping, because if Grandpa sees sprinkles all over the glass counter, he won't be pleased. He'll say, "Is that counter eating those sprinkles?" So the first thing I did was wipe down the counter, which was already clean.

"Ugh," whispered Kelsey, "it's the East twins."

The East twins were running up to the case and

putting their fingers all over the glass front. The two boys were adorable, but every time they came in, they made a huge mess.

"Hi, Mrs. East," said Kelsey. "What can we get you today?"

Mrs. East always looked like she'd just run through a windstorm. There were always papers coming out of her bag, and her clothes were usually wrinkled or stained.

But she was really nice, and after Mom died she made us a lot of dinners and brought them over. She even came over with a picnic lunch one day for me and Sky and took us to the park.

"Oh, let me get the boys settled here," she said, lifting them into chairs. "Jason, please stop hitting your brother!"

"That one, that one!" the boys started yelling, waving their little hands at the donuts.

"Boys!" said Mrs. East. "Use your manners! And Christopher, stop screaming!"

The boys scrambled off their chairs and ran back to the counter. Luckily, there was no one else waiting, because it took them a full ten minutes to choose their donuts.

I had one hand over the chocolate iced one when Christopher yelled, "No, no, no, not that one!" and I had to move my hand around the shelf until it was hovering over the "right" one.

"Thank you," said Mrs. East. "You girls are amazingly patient! And I'm more frazzled today than usual. We just got back from vacation with my mom, and even though we love them, moms can be such a pain sometimes. Right, girls?"

She looked up as she was handing us the money for the donuts and froze. Her eyes went wide as she looked at me, remembering, and then her hand flew over her mouth.

Kelsey shifted from foot to foot nervously.

This happens a lot. People will say things and then be really scared that they said the wrong thing in front of you. Before Mom died, even when she was sick, all of a sudden everyone was really careful about what they said around me. For a month after Mom died, my friends wouldn't even talk about their moms in front of me.

I talked to Aunt Melissa about it, because she was who I went to for a lot of stuff these days.

"Honey, people are trying to be considerate. But

sometimes you have to help them, too," Aunt Melissa told me.

Poor Mrs. East looked a little like she might cry. Kelsey looked at me expectantly.

"Yeah, you should hear Kelsey complain about Aunt Melissa," I joked.

Kelsey opened the cash drawer and smiled. "Yeah, but she's got nothing on Nans, and you basically live with Nans."

We laughed, but Mrs. East still stood there, silent. I could tell she still felt awful.

"That'll be five fifty, please," said Kelsey, and Mrs. East suddenly looked down and realized she still had the donut money in her hand.

"Oh thank you, honey," she said.

She took the donuts to the boys, who shoved them into their mouths in five seconds flat. Then she walked back over and grabbed some extra napkins.

"Sometimes you take things for granted," she said to me, I guess as an apology. "How was your summer, Lindsay? You excited for your first day at Bellgrove Middle School? Oh and the big Fall Fling is soon, right? Did you do any dress shopping this summer?"

Fall Fling is, I guess, a big deal. It's the fall dance at

the middle school, and everybody goes. I think they go because there's not much else to do, but kids start talking about it around the Fourth of July.

My BFF, Casey, had already started looking online for a dress, and she's been poking me to go shopping. The thing is that shopping for school is a little weird these days. Usually Aunt Melissa takes me and Kelsey to the mall that's an hour and a half away and we stock up, or we just order stuff online.

"I'm not ready to start thinking about school," I said. "It's still summer!"

"You're right!" laughed Mrs. East. "You enjoy every last drop of summer!"

Then she went over to try to wipe the boys' faces, which were covered in donut icing. It was also in their hair.

"So did you pick out a dress yet?" I asked Kelsey.

"Not yet," she said. "I found a few online that Mom said she'd order so I can try them on. Here, I'll show you."

She grabbed her phone from behind the counter, which was a big no-no. Grandpa did not let anyone have a phone when they were "on the floor," which meant out in the open in the restaurant.

26

"You have to pay full attention!" he'd say.

I hated this rule, because if there was some downtime, it could get really boring.

Dad came over then. "Are you girls doing okay?" he asked, eyeing the mess the Easts were making.

"Yep," said Kelsey. "We've got it, Uncle Mike." She slipped her phone into her back pocket.

"Kelsey, you know the rule," said Dad. "And if Grandpa catches you, it won't be pretty."

"I asked to see her dress," I said, trying to cover for her.

"What dress?" asked Dad.

"The dress she might wear for Fall Fling."

Dad looked confused.

"Fall Fling is a big deal, Mike," said Aunt Melissa, who had come up behind him.

"Oh, so I guess . . . well . . . we'll have to get Lindsay a dress?" he said, and he sounded so scared we all laughed.

But I had kind of wondered about it. I mean, Aunt Melissa usually took me shopping for school clothes, but no one had mentioned dress shopping. There was one store in town that had some fancy stuff, and that's where Casey's mom would probably take her.

"It's covered, Mike," said Aunt Melissa. "You're a great brother, but I would never count on you to pick out a dress."

Dad looked relieved.

"So you bought me one?" I asked, confused.

"Nope," said Aunt Melissa. "Your grandma Mimi did. Actually, she bought ten."

"Mimi?" I asked. "*Ten* dresses?"

"Yes," said Aunt Melissa. "There's some store near her that specializes in this kind of thing. I think she originally bought a dozen, but I told her that was crazy, so she narrowed it down to ten."

"Ten?" yelped Dad.

"Well, she's only going to keep one," said Aunt Melissa. "Unless you can wear more than one dress at a time. Can you, Linds?" she asked, teasing.

"So wait," Dad said. "Lindsay's grandma picked out her dresses? Can't Lindsay pick out her own clothes?"

Aunt Melissa laughed. "Your grandmother has wonderful taste," she said to me. "But there's a lot to choose from, don't worry. We will make sure you love whatever you end up wearing. Plus, she's insisted on bringing them when she comes, so she'll—" She stopped midsentence. "Oops."

"When is she coming?" I asked.

"Melissa!" said Dad. Then he sighed. "Okay, Mimi is coming for a surprise visit. Or at least it was *supposed* to be a surprise. She wanted to be here for you guys on the first day of school."

That was a little weird.

"Well, you know, it's a big deal, especially because you're starting middle school. She wanted to be here," said Dad.

"We're going to have a little dress party," said Aunt Melissa. "Kelsey, Molly, Jenna, and I are coming, and Nans, of course. Plus Aunt Sabrina and Lily. And we thought we'd invite Casey, too."

Aunt Sabrina is married to Uncle Charlie, and she's my cousins Lily and Rich's mom.

"I'm not invited?" asked Dad.

"Definitely not," said Aunt Melissa. "We already have too many opinions with that crew."

"My little girl is going to a dance," said Dad, and he got a little teary.

"Is anyone working today or should we all have a cup of tea?" asked Grandpa, whispering loudly behind us.

"It's okay, Dad," said Aunt Melissa. "We just had

a five-minute family huddle about scheduling." She winked at us.

"Yep," said Dad, taking her cue. "And here's Lindsay reporting for her first day at Donut Dreams."

Grandpa beamed. "There's always room for family in the Park!" he bellowed. "Now get back to work, everyone!"

After we cleaned up from the East twins, which required sweeping and mopping the floor and cleaning the table and chairs they'd sat in, it was a little slow.

The lunchtime crew was getting busy on the other side of the restaurant, and I saw my cousins: Jenna, Kelsey's older sister, and Lily in their waitress uniforms, serving table after table.

Jenna, Lily, and Lily's older brother, Rich, were the only ones allowed to wait on tables, because they were old enough. Molly, Kelsey's other sister, was a runner, which meant she filled the glasses at the tables, brought extra ketchup or hot sauce if someone asked for it, and replaced a napkin if someone dropped it on the floor—stuff like that. Then Kelsey and I were on the Dream Team. One day Skylar would probably work here too.

We got a little busier after lunch, when people would buy a donut to go. Kelsey and I had a good rhythm together, with one of us putting the donuts in a bag and the other one ringing up the customers and keeping the line moving. (We knew some of the regulars' orders already.)

Principal Clarke, who was the principal of the middle school where I'd be going, smiled at me as she came up in line.

"Well, I think you'll be joining us soon, Lindsay," she said.

"Yes, ma'am," I said. "Looking forward to it!"

"Oh, I can't wait to have you. It's going to be a great year!" She watched as Kelsey packed her dozen donuts. "I'm headed over for a meeting now and thought I'd sweeten up some of the teachers!"

"Well, donuts usually do the trick!" I said.

I wondered about the teachers. Some of them were friends of Mom's. But even if you know someone, they can act totally different when they're in front of a classroom.

After Principal Clarke left, Kelsey whispered, "The sweetest donut in the world won't sweeten Mrs. Gable up."

I giggled because she was right.

Mrs. Gable taught at the middle school and also happened to be my next-door neighbor. She was what Nans called "a prune." She was always complaining about things and was never really friendly.

Dad always shoveled her walk and helped rake her leaves anyway, which I thought was nice, since she was always yelling over the fence that Sky and I were making too much noise in the backyard.

Eventually, we slowed down again. We had to run an inventory report, which showed how many donuts and which kinds we'd sold, so that we could plan better and not run out. But since Uncle Charlie made the system automatic, we did that in about a minute.

Kelsey and I leaned on the counter. "Are you nervous about middle school?" she asked. "Because it's different."

"Not really," I said. "How different can it be?"

"You wouldn't think that much, but it is," said Kelsey. "At least that's what Jenna tells me."

I raised an eyebrow.

Jenna always acts like she knows everything, and Kelsey and her sister Molly always believe everything she says. Since Jenna is already in high school, they act like she's the queen. Jenna's always been supersweet to me and I love her, but sometimes her know-it-all attitude can get a little irritating.

"So according to Jenna, how is it different?" I asked.

"Well," said Kelsey, "for one thing there's more homework. And you move around from class to class a lot more."

I expected those things. I mean, last year Mrs. Graves told us every single day, "You'll see next year in middle school . . . the teachers won't tolerate anything less than your best. And there will be a lot more work!"

And moving around from class to class? It might be nice to get a bigger change of scenery. I still wasn't worried.

"So what kind of dresses do you think Mimi picked out?" asked Kelsey.

"Don't know," I said, starting to wonder myself. "There are lots more stores near where she lives, so she probably has a range, right?"

Kelsey shrugged. "Well, there's definitely more there than there are here. I mean, there's only one dress store in town. So you're lucky, because your dress will probably be really different from everyone else's."

"Yeah," I said, perking up. "That's true, and pretty cool."

Dad came over just then and whispered, "Elbows off the counters, girls, and look alive . . . or Grandpa will eat you alive!"

We giggled and stood up straight.

The main restaurant always had customers, but Donut Dreams definitely had busy times and not very busy times. We swept the floor again and moved the donuts around on the shelf, but there wasn't a whole lot to do.

I felt bad because my other cousins were running around the restaurant. It wasn't East boys' level of crazy, but my friend Hannah's three year-old brother, Tristan, could be a handful, and he kept dropping his silverware on the floor. Molly would have to scoot over, pick it up, and bring him a new fork or spoon.

Mrs. Wood was always really nice, but even she was getting tired of Tristan's behavior.

"For goodness' sake!" she yelped. "No more forks! That's it!"

Molly froze, a new fork in hand.

"Molly, honey, you can leave that with me, and

when Tristan starts behaving, he can have his fork," Mrs. Wood said.

Molly put the fork on the napkin, as Grandpa taught us to do, and skittered away. She shot us a look across the room and rolled her eyes.

I wasn't really sure why Molly was a runner and Kelsey and I were "on the counter," but that's the way it was set up.

Maybe because Molly is technically a little older than us, even though we're all in the same grade at school. Molly was adopted, and right when she came home with Aunt Melissa and Uncle Chris, they found out they were having a baby, and that was Kelsey.

But even though Molly is ten months older, a fact she likes to point out a lot, Kelsey and Molly are pretty much the same age. Grandpa used to call them the "almost twins" until last year, when Molly threw a fit about it.

"That one has sass," Nans said, when Molly exploded at Grandpa.

"She has spunk, and we love her for it," said Aunt Melissa. "And she's right. The girls aren't twins."

Molly's spunk might be the other reason that she wasn't working behind a counter. I could totally see her saying to the East twins, "Just pick a donut already!"

Plus, Molly has a lot of energy, and she doesn't mind running around.

Donut Dreams closed at six o'clock every day. Nans said you couldn't really keep donuts fresh past that point, and not a lot of people eat donuts at night, which is a strange but true fact. It got really, really slow in the afternoon, so I took my break.

When I came back to the counter, I worried a little bit because in our family we always talk about "business" and whether "business is slow" or "business is good." Busy was always good, slow was not.

Jenna dropped off a tray full of food to the Woods' table, then came over to us.

"How are you doing, girls?" she asked. "Can you spare a cinnamon donut? I'm starving."

Kelsey reached into the case and put a cinnamon donut on a napkin.

"Oh, that was such hard work," said Jenna. "You sure you guys can handle this job?"

"Maybe," I said.

Jenna laughed. "*You* can definitely handle it. My sister Kelsey is not a fan of working."

"Well, it's the end of summer," Kelsey whined. "Everyone else is at the lake today!"

"They've been at the lake all summer!" said Jenna. "How is today any different?" She had a point.

"Because it's like the last stretch of summer that we should hold on to before we go back to school."

Jenna gave her a look.

"Trust me, Kelsey," she said. "You aren't missing anything."

Jenna and I agreed on life here. Jenna was always bored and always planning.

"That one's got her eye on the door," Nans always said, and Aunt Melissa would sigh.

"She has big dreams. But she'll come back," she would reply. "They always do. Just wait and see."

But with Jenna I wasn't so sure. She was constantly talking about moving to Los Angeles, where the weather was beautiful all year. Jenna studied really hard and was always talking about her grades and whether they were good enough to get into a good college.

Jenna took the donut into the kitchen to eat. That was another rule here: no eating on the floor.

I know, it's crazy, right? I mean, we make and serve

food but can't eat in front of the customers. You'd think they'd want us to advertise that the food is so delicious we eat it ourselves. But on the other hand, I guess it wouldn't be good for a customer to ask us a question and us to answer with a mouthful of donut.

"Is Mom taking you home after work?" she asked Kelsey.

"I think so," said Kelsey. "But we have to wait for Molly's shift to end too. That's another hour."

"Well, maybe Uncle Mike can drop you off," said Jenna. "I think Lily is driving me, or maybe Rich."

Lily and Rich were both older, and both of them had their driver's licenses. Rich was the oldest cousin, and Skylar was the youngest. Nans joked that her two grandsons bookended the girls in between.

At big family dinners, I always felt a little sorry for Rich because he was definitely outnumbered, but Sky loved him and followed him everywhere.

Finally it was closing time, which meant we had to clear the shelves, clean the counters, empty the trash, and close out the register. Grandpa didn't like us to close out until actual closing time, because he said it turned away customers if they thought they needed to rush before you went home.

So Kelsey and I watched until the clock said six o'clock on the dot, and then we sprang into close-mode. We made a good team and played Rock-Paper-Scissors to see who had trash duty, which was the worst.

You had to empty the trash, throw the bag into the Dumpster in the back, then lug the trash can into the parking lot and hose it down. Even though there should have been just napkins and cups, there was always something really gross in the trash can. One time I had to scrape out gum, and it was awful.

"Great job today, girls!" said Dad as we signed out.

Everyone who worked at the Park recorded when they started working and when they stopped. Aunt Melissa was a stickler for records, and she was always complaining that someone didn't log out.

"Ready to do it again tomorrow?" asked Grandpa.

Kelsey sighed. "Ugh."

"Hey, young lady," said Grandpa. "You should consider yourself lucky to have a job!"

"Grandpa, I am!" she said, pouting. "But it's the last few days before school starts!"

"And then what happens?" Grandpa teased. "The big bad school monster comes out?"

Kelsey laughed. "Grandpa! We will have homework and we have to sit in school all day and not do fun things like swim in the lake and stay up late!"

"Oh, my poor, poor granddaughter," said Grandpa. "Are you allergic to work? Because if you are, we may need to kick you out of the family!"

"Dad!" said Aunt Melissa. "You can never kick anyone out of this family!"

"Especially not me!" said Kelsey.

She was right. Kelsey was always Grandpa's favorite. It wasn't like he didn't love all of us, but there was something about Kelsey that allowed her to act in a way that would have made Grandpa very prickly with the rest of us.

Nans said that it was because Kelsey was named after Grandpa's mother Katherine, and that Kelsey was very much like her.

"I'm taking the girls home," said Dad. "Melissa is waiting for Molly to finish her shift. I'll be back soon."

Kelsey and I followed him out to the car. We had been inside for most of the day, so the sun felt especially hot and bright. We blinked as we walked.

"Melissa said I could drop you at the lake if you wanted, Kels," said Dad.

"I can't go like this!" Kelsey said. "I'm in my work clothes."

"But it's just the lake," Dad said.

"Uncle Mike, you can't go to the lake in work clothes," said Kelsey. "Besides, everyone is probably headed home now anyway."

Dad shrugged. Our town isn't that big, but it's kind of spread out in parts, so there are a bunch of us who live five minutes away and then there are people like Kelsey, who live on the other side of the lake.

Some people have boats and just row or drive across the lake instead of taking a car. There have been a lot of stories about kids taking boats out at night, and Dad has already hammered it into our heads that it's too dangerous to do that.

At Kelsey's house, Uncle Chris opened the door when he heard the car pull up and waved to us.

"See you tomorrow," I said to Kelsey as she opened the car door, and she sighed.

It was still pretty sticky and hot. I guess a lot of people were on vacation, because the town seemed quiet, which was kind of nice.

"So how was your first day?" asked Dad as we drove away from Kelsey's house.

"Pretty good," I said. "A little slow."

"Yeah," said Dad. "Time of year. You'll see, it will speed up. That's when the days go a lot faster."

Dad and I drove in the quiet. It was nice having this time with just him, without Skylar or Nans or Grandpa or a million other family members. I actually didn't mind the slow pace of the day. I hoped things didn't speed up too quickly.

Chapter Three
My BFF Is Back!

I didn't have to worry about things going quickly, because even though the next day was kind of slow at Donut Dreams, it had a nice rhythm.

Kelsey and I were pretty good about splitting the "ick" stuff, as we called it, like hosing down the mat behind the counter or making sure the chairs were clean underneath (you wouldn't believe). I liked chatting with the customers, and I knew almost everyone who came in.

After a flurry of morning customers, I had a second to sip some water. I was itching to check my phone because I knew my best friend, Casey, was coming home today, and I couldn't wait to see her.

But even though my phone was in my apron

pocket, Grandpa had been especially vigilant this morning, and I didn't want him to catch me using it.

Grandpa has been telling every customer that he now has six out of seven grandchildren working at the restaurant.

"One more and it's a full house!" he'll say.

I cannot imagine Sky working . . . at all. He'd probably complain the entire time and try to eat all the donuts.

On the one hand, it is nice to work with my family because we help each other out. One day, while here after school, Lily dropped a huge tray she was carrying, and it made such a loud crashing sound that everyone stopped talking and stared at her.

In a flash Molly, Jenna, and Rich ran over to help her, and they got everything up off the ground in record time.

Another time crazy Mr. Brown, who is known to have a temper, yelled at Jenna for not toasting his bread well enough, and Grandpa walked over and said, "Hey, Ed, are you yelling at one of my favorite granddaughters over a tuna sandwich?" and calmed him down right away.

Family always has your back, and while Grandpa

can be tough, he is also pretty protective of us.

I was busy wiping down the counter when I heard someone scream, "I'M BAAAAAACK!" That could only be one person: Casey, my best friend in the entire world! We've been friends since we were born, because we were born exactly one day apart and were in the hospital together.

She has gone to sleepaway camp for the past few summers, which generally makes me miserable because I miss her so much. At her camp you can't have computers or phones, so she can't e-mail me, let alone text me, and I hate not being able to talk to her. Casey sometimes sends postcards, but it's not the same thing.

I spun around and Casey charged at me, hugging me over the counter.

"So how much did you miss me?" she asked.

"A lot!" I said.

"I need to know everything that I missed this summer!" she said.

I blinked. "Seriously? You missed nothing, Casey. You know that!"

"Really?" she asked. "I was hoping something exciting might have happened."

"Um . . . no," I said.

"Well, you got a job!" she said, grinning. "Spin around and let me see your uniform."

I spun around, pointing to the DREAM TEAM on the back of the shirt.

"Nice, nice," she said.

"Casey!" Kelsey squealed, coming back from the kitchen.

She was so happy to see Casey, she almost dropped the tray she was carrying.

"I have returned!" said Casey dramatically.

"Wow, you look different," said Kelsey.

I looked at Casey. She did look different.

First of all, she was wearing a little makeup, which was surprising because I knew her mom hadn't let her wear any before the summer. She also seemed to be a few inches taller.

She was wearing shorts and a T-shirt, but she looked . . . well, more put together or something, not like she just threw clothes on, which I knew for a fact was what she usually did. And they were usually clothes she had stashed under her bed. She had on a cute pair of sandals, and her toes were painted purple with glitter. Her hair, which was usually in a ponytail, was down and bouncy and curled like she'd just had it styled.

"Did you just get your hair cut?" I asked.

"No, but I used a blow-dryer," she said.

"You used a blow-dryer in August?" I asked.

Normally, I only blow-dried my hair when it was freezing cold and Nans was yelling that I couldn't possibly go outside with wet hair or it would freeze on my head.

"I have been dying for those sandals!" said Kelsey. "But Mom won't let me get them. Did your feet grow too or can I borrow them?"

"Kelsey, are you taking the shoes off poor Casey as soon as she returns to our fine town?" asked Dad, who was grinning.

He loved Casey and came out from the kitchen to say hello the minute he heard her voice. "Hey, Case. Did you have any big summer adventures?"

"I did!" said Casey very seriously. "I had some monumental softball games."

Then she burst out laughing. "It was great. I had a lot of fun, and it was nice to get away."

I'll bet, I thought.

I had asked Dad if I could go to summer camp,

but he wasn't too into the idea. I made a note to myself to start bugging him about it early for next summer. Maybe he'd change his mind next year.

Casey's phone buzzed, and she looked at it with a giant smile on her face. I had never seen her smile like that before.

"Who's bugging you besides me?" I asked.

"Oh, just someone I met at camp," she said. "His name is Matt."

Matt?

"You have a boyfriend?" Kelsey yelped.

"He's not really my . . . ," said Casey. "Well, he's kind of . . . I don't know. Summer's over, and he lives far away, so . . ."

My head was spinning a little. We barely spoke to boys. I mean, we spoke to them, but we had never looked at our boy *friends* as potential boyfriend material.

"You came home from camp with a boyfriend?" Dad asked. "Well, that's it. Lindsay is never, ever going to camp now!" He laughed.

"Daaaad," I said, crossing my arms.

"Who has a boyfriend?" asked Lily, whizzing by. "Oh, Casey!"

She gave Casey a squeeze and winked. "Well, I'd say that sounds like you had a good summer!"

"I did!" said Casey, and then her mom came in.

"Hey, I said you could run in, honey," Mrs. Peters said, exasperated.

Then she saw me. "Oh, Linds, I've missed you!"

"You missed Lindsay more than you missed me!" said Casey, all huffy.

"Well, she doesn't give me as hard a time as you do," said Mrs. Peters, embracing me in a big hug.

Mrs. Peters takes Casey to camp and then goes to visit her mother, Casey's grandma, for the summer. Casey's grandma moved to Arizona so she could be warm all year, which drives Mrs. Peters crazy because they don't get to see her a lot.

"How is Granny?" I asked.

"Good, good," said Mrs. Peters. "She sends her love and said we should all come see her when it snows, because she'll be at the pool!"

"Ooh, that could be fun," Casey said, her mind already whirling.

"Casey, the dog is going nuts in the car," said Mrs. Peters. "We were on our way back home, but you know we *had* to stop and see Lindsay first!"

"Well, I am the main attraction of the town," I said, grinning.

"Of course you are," Casey said. "Okay, I'll come over later."

"Casey, you just got home, and Dad and I would like to have dinner together as a family!" said Mrs. Peters.

"Okay," said Casey. "After dinner, then!"

"Can I have you for twenty-four hours?" asked Mrs. Peters. "Seriously, Casey. You and Lindsay have plenty of time to catch up."

"Fine!" said Casey. "At least I can text now. I'll TTYL, Linds!"

I gave her another quick hug, and she was halfway out the door before she whipped back around.

"Oh my gosh, I missed the donuts almost as much as you! We need four, please!"

I smiled, because I knew that she liked cinnamon, Gabby liked old-fashioned, and Mr. and Mrs. Peters liked powdered jelly. I carefully put them in the bag.

"Those are on the house!" Dad called. "Welcome back, Casey. We missed you!"

"Thank you," said Casey. "I promise I'll eat them all, even the ones for my parents!"

Dad laughed, and Casey and her mom rushed out.

I was so glad to have my BFF home. I missed having Casey as my go-to, because she just always knew what I was thinking or how I felt about things, and I didn't need to explain everything to her. She just got me.

On the other hand, Casey seemed different. I mean, a boyfriend was a big deal. Who was this guy Matt?

Maybe Jenna was right. Maybe middle school *was* going to be different.

Chapter Four
Early Dismissal

At eleven o'clock the next Monday morning, Dad sauntered up to the counter and asked if I wanted the rest of the day off.

"Really?" I asked, surprised.

"Yep," said Dad. "We leave at noon."

"Wait," I said. "Leave for where? To do what?"

"Special surprise!" Dad called over his shoulder.

"No fair!" said Kelsey. "I get stuck here and you get a day off?"

I didn't know what to say, because it actually didn't sound very fair.

"You can leave too," said Rich, who was walking over wearing a Dream Team tee. "I'm covering the counter from noon to six."

"Yes!" Kelsey yelled, and pumped her fist. "Lake bound!"

The next hour actually sped up because we were crowded, and I felt bad about turning over the counter to Rich. I guess more people were coming back from vacation because the Park, Donut Dreams, and even the town itself was busier.

My next customers were Mrs. Ellis and her daughter Elizabeth, aka Wetsy Betsy. I mean, it's terrible that we're friends and I still think of her as Wetsy Betsy, but I can't get it out of my head.

It's not like anyone really calls her Wetsy Betsy, except for Mitchell Stewart, who is kind of a bully anyway. "Hey, Wetsy!" he'll say when he sees her. She just ignores him, but I'm sure it bothers her.

"Hi, Lindsay!" Elizabeth said.

I smiled back at her. "Hey, Elizabeth."

"How has your summer been, Lindsay?" asked Mrs. Ellis. "Did you enjoy the rec classes as much as Elizabeth did?"

Elizabeth and I—along with most of the kids—went to the camp that the town ran for a few hours every morning. We hung out at rec because we both liked the art classes, and Elizabeth was really good at ceramics. She helped me work the wheel so I could make a bowl for Nans.

"It was pretty good," I said. "I wish summer was twice as long, though!"

"I do too!" Mrs. Ellis said. She worked at the high school, so she had most of the summer off too.

The thing I've learned about working in a restaurant is that people generally want to talk to you. I guess it's polite? They can't just say, "Give me that donut," so they say, "Oh, it's so hot out that I decided to treat myself to a donut and cool iced tea to wash it down. Isn't it just so hot?" So I end up talking about the weather a lot.

"Pretty soon it will be Fall Fling, and I can't believe you girls are starting up with all that soon!" said Mrs. Ellis.

Ugh, Fall Fling again.

When you live in a town where nothing ever happens, little things are a big deal. But I wasn't sure what she meant by "starting up with all that." Starting up with what? Getting dressed up? We did that already on holidays and for family things. Last year was Nans and Grandpa's fortieth anniversary, and we all had to get really dressed up. Dad even wore a suit.

"Enjoy the last of summer, dear!" Mrs. Ellis said.

Elizabeth waved. "See you at the lake!" she said.

Here's the thing: everyone goes to the lake. But nothing really happens at the lake. We all take our towels and phones and some of us bring books, and everyone sits around talking to each other. If it's really hot, we'll jump in, and some kids play volleyball in the water, but mostly it's a lot of just hanging out. On a beautiful day it's really nice, but it also gets pretty boring by the end of the summer, with all of us running out of conversation and just staring out into the lake.

The lake was a big deal this year because it was the first year that me and my friends were allowed to go without an adult. There were lifeguards there, but the lifeguards were mostly the older brothers and sisters of my friends.

Everyone is always so intent on being there, though. It's like buying tickets to a show, but there's nothing on the stage, you know? Everyone just ends up watching each other, even though we've all been staring at each other for years.

I guess there's one thing that has changed. When we used to go with an adult, we'd sit with them. Kids hung out with their families. Since we're going with friends now, we're all arranged in slightly different circles. All the middle school kids sit together with the high school kids mostly at one end of the lake.

Without Casey this summer, I mostly sat with Kelsey and her BFF, Sophia. Sometimes Molly would hang out with us too. I guess it is weird that Molly and Kelsey have totally separate friends, since they are sisters and in the same grade, but they are so different that it makes sense.

Kelsey likes to think she's friends with everybody, and that everyone likes her. She always cares about what people think, and she is obsessed with being in on everything.

I still remember the fit she threw in third grade when she wasn't invited to Anna's birthday party. It turns out she was; Anna had just accidentally dropped Kelsey's invitation on her way to school.

Molly is much more of a free spirit. She could not care less what people think about her, and pretty much always says what's on her mind, which does tend to get her in trouble. Nans says she has absolutely no filter from her brain to her mouth. But Molly is also a lot of fun, and she's the first one to organize a kayak race across the lake or a s'mores contest to see who can build the biggest one.

She's really good with little kids, too, so they're always running over to her at the lake. Molly says that when she's old enough she's going to babysit instead of working at the Park, but Aunt Melissa says, "Molly, family first. If we need you, we need to know you'll be there."

There are only twenty-five girls in my grade, so the truth is, even if we split ourselves up, we are all kind of forced to hang out together. There are a ton of cousins and one set of twins, so there are also a lot of people related to each other. My point is, you can't really get away from anyone. Sure, I'm going to avoid some of the meaner girls, but at some point I'm going to be in class or on a team with them.

"Okay, Rich," said Dad. "You got this?"

"I got it," said Rich, eyeing the door because a bunch of his friends from the soccer team had come in and were swarming the counter.

"Hiiiiiii, Lindsay!" called Mason R.

There were three Masons on Rich's team, so they went by Mason R., Mason L., and Mason B.

Mason R. leaned over the counter. "Hey, can you

give me a dozen donuts even if I only pay for a half dozen?" He smiled.

I smiled back. "Nope," I said.

Mason R. laughed.

Rich's friends always tried to get us to give them free donuts. Uncle Charlie brought them to every game, and each of those guys ate about four. Uncle Charlie joked that the soccer team would eat us out of business.

"Get out of here, Linds," said Rich, "before they try to get you to sell them the whole case at half price."

Dad was waiting for me off to the side of the counter. "Okay, Pops," he said to Grandpa. "We're off. I'll see you later tonight!"

Grandpa gave me a quick hug. "Are you sure your grandma Mimi's plane is on time?" he asked, looking at his phone.

I looked at Dad. "Mimi's plane?"

"Pops!" Dad yelled.

I giggled. I guess Grandpa had just ruined some sort of surprise!

Chapter Five
Grandma Mimi

"What?" said Grandpa. "She already knows her grandma Mimi is coming!"

I laughed. "Well, I didn't know she was coming *today*!" I said.

"For goodness' sake," said Dad, throwing up his hands. "No one in this family can keep a secret!"

Grandpa looked around. "Well, no one told me this was still a secret. They just told me her whole trip was a secret but Melissa spilled!"

Dad shook his head. "Okay, Lindsay," he said. "I thought it would be nice to pick up Grandma Mimi from the airport, so we have a ways to go. Let's get out of here before Grandpa and the family also tell you what I'm getting you for your birthday and every other secret we still have." Then he laughed. It was hard to stay mad at Grandpa for long.

The airport is about two and a half hours away, in St. Louis. Sometimes Dad takes us to St. Louis for a weekend, which is a lot of fun. It's so crazy different there, with so much more to do. It's weird that you can get in a car, drive, and end up someplace that's so different from where you started.

"I figure we'll get there in time to pick up Grandma Mimi," Dad said, heading out to the highway. "Then we'll have an early dinner and head back."

"We're having dinner in the city?" I said, realizing I still had my Donut Dreams T-shirt on with a pair of shorts.

Dad usually wore a nice button-down shirt to work with pants and nice shoes, so he always looked a little dressed up to me. And Mimi was always, always dressed up. No matter where she was, she always had lipstick on and some kind of jewelry. I tried to picture Mimi on the plane like a lot of other grandmas, wearing sweatpants and a sweatshirt, but I just couldn't do it.

"Mimi wants to take you on a little surprise excursion in St. Louis," said Dad. "And Uncle Charlie wants me to meet with one of our vendors for the restaurant, so I'll leave you guys to it. Then I'll pick you both up for dinner. Okay?"

"Sounds great!" I said.

Some people might think it's strange that I am looking forward to hanging out with my grandma, but I love being with Mimi. It was the rest of the family that sometimes annoyed me.

Dad is always on time for everything, so of course we got to the airport a little early. I watched people lugging bags or rolling suitcases, and I wondered where they'd been or what adventure they were heading off to.

"What's one place that you've never been that you'd like to see?" I asked Dad.

Dad and I did this a lot, asking things like, *If you could eat only one thing for twenty-four hours, what food would you choose?*

"Hmm," Dad said. "Well, Europe was wonderful, but if it has to be someplace I've never been, I think I'd love to go to Japan."

I nodded. I always forget Dad had traveled a lot with Mom, before she got sick.

Mom lived in France for a year during college,

and when Dad went to visit her, they traveled all over Europe.

"But you know I'm not a big traveler," said Dad. "I like being home. It's fun to see other countries, but I miss home when I'm away."

"Did Mom miss home when she was living in France?" I asked.

"Well, she definitely missed her family and her friends," said Dad. "And me!" He laughed. "But I think she liked learning how people lived in different cities. To some extent she had to learn how people lived in our town too."

I thought about that. "You mean like how we pronounce certain words?"

"Well, that, yes," said Dad. "But also that everyone eats dinner early or that people think it's rude if you don't say hello when you see them out and about, that kind of thing. When she first moved here, she could not get used to the fact that people would just walk in the front door without knocking first. For about six months, she screamed when anyone came into the house."

I laughed. "Well, to be fair, people only walk in if you've invited them over or are expecting them.

It's not like we just randomly walk into each other's houses!"

"Of course not!" said Dad. "But even then. One time when Casey's mom came over, she startled Mom so much that Mom dropped an entire platter of meatballs and spaghetti she was making for dinner. There was red sauce everywhere . . . even on the ceiling."

I cracked up. "Wow, that sounds like a mess!"

"It was," said Dad. "There was sauce in her hair and dripping from above. And we all laughed at her, and she did not like that one bit!"

I giggled. I was used to seeing Mom covered in paint but not sauce.

Then I spotted Mimi striding toward us. She was hard to miss. Mimi doesn't exactly look like a grandma, or at least not like what most of my friends' grandmas look like.

She wears bright red lipstick that's always perfect—it never smudges, even when she eats (and I've watched her!). She is always what she calls "smartly dressed," which means she's usually in pants, with a nice top and a jacket and heels.

I've never seen her wear jeans, and the only time

she wears sneakers is when she goes for a run, which she does every day. Dad sometimes teases Mimi about wearing sweats, but we all know she doesn't own one sweatshirt.

Today Mimi had on these cool sunglasses and a scarf wrapped around her neck, I guess because she was cold on the plane. Her feet, as always, made a *click, click, click* sound with her shoes.

"Baby girl!" Mimi cried out, and grabbed me for a big hug.

She smelled like flowers. She took off her sunglasses and propped them on top of her head.

"Let me take a good look at you. Oh, you are even more beautiful than ever, and . . ." She looked at Dad. "She's the spitting image of Amy, isn't she?"

Dad smiled. "Well, she's Lindsay, so she looks like Lindsay to me," he said.

"Oh, you know what I mean!" said Mimi. "Lindsay, you look more and more like your beautiful mother each time I see you."

She looked at me for a minute longer. I wondered if she was imagining me as Mom, or Mom with my head. Or Mom's head on me.

"Good to see you, Mike!" Mimi said then, giving

Dad a long hug. "You seem to be faring well."

"I am!" said Dad.

"You know I would have been happy to drive out to you," said Mimi.

"Don't be silly," said Dad as we walked toward the exit of the terminal. "Happy to give you some company on the trip. And we like our city trips, don't we, Linds?" He winked. "It's good practice for when Lindsay leaves us and moves to the big town!"

"Oh?" said Mimi. "There's so much to catch up on! Lindsay, I want to hear everything you're up to! And how is my sweetie Skylar? Did you leave him at home? I was hoping he'd join us!"

Dad grabbed Mimi's bag and we piled into the car. "Well, I didn't think he'd last while you went out," he said as he started up the car engine. "Unless you take him shopping for video games."

"Well, I'm happy to shop for Sky, too," said Mimi, "but all he wears are those terrible athletic clothes. He looks like he's going to the gym all the time!"

"Marla, that's what all the boys wear," said Dad.

Mimi shook her head. "I bought him some button-down shirts," she said. "And a few pairs of pants."

Dad rolled his eyes and smiled at me in the rearview mirror.

"Where are we going today?" I asked Mimi. "Dad said it's a surprise."

Mimi nodded and smiled. "Oh, it is," she said. "It definitely is."

Chapter Six
A Day at the Museum

Mimi typed an address into her phone, and we were off to the St. Louis Art Museum. Before I knew it, Mimi was ready to march me into the museum, but not without first touching up her makeup and hair in the car.

"Oh, I'm such a mess from traveling!" she said.

I tried not to giggle as I looked at Dad, because not one hair on Mimi's head was out of place.

Dad pulled up in front of the museum and let us out.

"Have fun," he shouted as we waved goodbye.

At the entrance, Mimi asked a man at the information desk for "a docent named Ellen Colbert."

The man picked up the phone and made a call.

"She'll be right down," he said.

I turned to Mimi. "Docent?" I asked.

Mimi smiled. "A docent is a museum guide."

A few minutes later a woman came to the desk and said, "Marla?"

"Yes!" said Grandma. "But you can call me Mimi! And are you Ellen?"

Ellen nodded. "I am! Jenny told me you were coming with your granddaughter."

I admired Ellen's black suit and silky white blouse. She wore black patent-leather pumps, and tiny little diamond stud earrings twinkled in her ears. She looked dressed up, yet she still managed to appear comfortable at the same time. Not an easy look to pull off.

Mimi shook Ellen's hand.

"This is my beautiful granddaughter Lindsay," she said, tucking my hair behind my ear. "Look at that gorgeous face!"

"Mimi!" I said, and I could feel my face getting hot.

Ellen laughed. "Oh, that's what grandmas do!"

She led us into the museum and started pointing out all the different paintings.

It was incredible. Even though Mom was an artist, I had never been to an art museum before.

Ellen smiled at me. "We have something here your grandmother has been eager to show you," she said. "She's been calling me nearly every day, asking, 'Is it still on? We didn't miss it, did we?'"

I looked up at Mimi questioningly. She didn't say anything.

Ellen laughed. "I think it's time to tell her, Mimi!"

Mimi nodded and took me by the hand.

"There's a special exhibit here this month," she said. "I'm just so glad I was able to get you here in time before it ended."

Then we walked down a hallway and there was a sign that read, THE ST. LOUIS ART MUSEUM IS PROUD TO HONOR CLAUDE MONET. EXHIBITION ON LOAN FROM THE NATIONAL GALLERY OF ART, WASHINGTON, DC. There was a security guard at the entrance who smiled and nodded at us as we walked in.

I gasped. Monet was my mom's absolute favorite artist. When I walked into the exhibition, I felt like I was dreaming.

"I'm sure your mom must have talked about Monet to you," Mimi said, smiling.

"Oh, you know, just . . . all the time," I said. "I know he painted by observing and using his own thoughts and emotions in his art, instead of drawing things exactly as they were in real life. Is that right?"

Ellen was nodding. She was also smiling from ear to ear.

"Very good! Yes, it's called impressionism, Lindsay," she said.

I walked over to one painting that caught my eye. It was called *Palazzo da Mula, Venice*. It was wonderful. I felt as if I could dip my hand into the cool blue water.

"Mom always talked about Monet and the way he painted water," I said.

Mimi tapped me on the shoulder. "Let me show you one of your mom's favorites," she said.

It was called *Woman with a Parasol—Madame Monet and Her Son*. It was a woman walking through a field of flowers, holding a parasol, with a little boy walking close to her.

As I looked at it, I took a deep breath.

"It's so . . . soothing, isn't it?" I said. "The puffy white clouds, the way her scarf is gently blowing in the breeze . . . I love how everything is so soft, and a little blurry." I gave a little happy sigh. "I could look at this for hours."

"You know, when Monet was alive, his work was criticized," Ellen said.

"Why?" I said. "How could someone not like this?" I pointed to the painting.

"Some critics said Monet's work was blurry not by choice, but because his eyesight was failing," Ellen explained. She shook her head. "They just wanted to criticize his work, instead of seeing the beauty behind it." She sighed. "Monet is one of my favorites too."

"Which goes to show you should do whatever you want when it comes to art," Mimi said. "Paint how you love to paint, write what you love to write, sing what you want to sing!"

She turned to me. "The point is, you're never going to make everybody happy, Lindsay, so it's important that you make *you* happy."

I nodded. "Thanks, Mimi."

Of course all this made me think of my mom. She always painted what made her happy. I pictured her sitting by her easel, softly humming as she mixed colors from her palette.

I remembered one time when she had just finished a painting; I caught her looking at the final product, her head tilted slightly to one side, with a small, satisfied smile on her face. "I can never get it exactly the way I see it in my mind, Linds," she told me. "But this one is close."

Monet painted a lot of water lilies, but there were other paintings I found equally wonderful. Fishing boats, sailboats, cathedrals: they were all beautiful to me.

After I made sure I had looked at every single one, Mimi called Dad to come pick us up, and told him we were going to make a quick stop at the gift shop first. Mimi bought me an art book all about Monet's paintings. It was pretty expensive.

We met up with Dad and got into the car, and the minute he saw the bag from the gift shop, Dad immediately whipped out his wallet, thinking I had asked Mimi to buy the pricey art book for me.

But Mimi waved her hand, shooing him away, saying it was a gift and her treat.

After some protest, Dad eventually put his wallet away. "But I'm paying for dinner," he said. "No arguments. It's not up for discussion."

Mimi nodded seriously. "Yes. Food I'll let you pay for," she said. And we all laughed.

Dad and Mimi and I stopped at a restaurant Dad wanted to try for dinner, and he went to talk to the manager while Mimi and I settled into a booth.

"I worked up an appetite," said Mimi.

I realized I was pretty hungry too. I looked at the menu, which was huge, and everything sounded good.

"Okay," said Dad, sliding into the other side of the table. "There are a few things I'd like to try, so let me know if there's anything that catches your eye. Otherwise I'll order for everyone."

"That makes it easy," said Mimi, and she slapped her menu shut and slid it to Dad.

Dad ordered enough food for about ten people.

"Uh, Mike, it's just the three of us, right?" asked Mimi.

"It's market research!" said Dad.

It was strange to be in a restaurant that wasn't the Park. I noticed how busy the staff was, and, because it was a big restaurant, they really had to move fast to get from the kitchen to the tables.

It was also weird to be out to dinner and not see one person we knew. I wondered if you could spend a whole day in a city without seeing anyone you had ever met before. You would be totally anonymous.

I wondered if that was good or bad. You could pretty much do what you wanted to do, but then again, if you didn't show up somewhere, would anyone know? What if you needed help and didn't know anyone to ask? What if you just wanted to see a friendly face but all you saw were strangers?

It was also a little weird being someplace with just Mimi and Dad. After Mom died, it seemed like three of us (me, Skylar, Dad), went everywhere together.

When we were a family of four, I didn't really notice when Mom was out or Skylar was off doing something. And since Dad worked a lot, there were a lot of times it was just Skylar, me, and Mom.

Now I'm always aware of where Dad and Skylar are, and it's like I'm constantly looking around for Sky if he's not with us. If I moved to the city, it would just be Dad and Sky back home.

For some reason that thought made my throat feel a little funny. Maybe without the two of them, I would be lonely.

Dad must have read my mind, because he said, "Ah, it's strange not to have Skylar here, but Mimi, you should consider this your last meal with no whining while you're visiting."

Mimi laughed. "Oh, Sky is a good kid," she said. "I can't wait to see him. But today is about Lindsay!

Tell me about middle school. Are you excited?"

Here we go again, I thought.

"Not really," I said. "It's a new school but the same kids, so not much is different."

"Oh!" said Mimi, surprised. "Your mom spoke so highly about the school, though. It has wonderful programs, especially for art. And some of her friends still teach there, right?"

I nodded.

"Well, Carla teaches there," Dad said. "You remember her, right, Mimi? And Laurie is still the assistant principal."

"Laurie is Casey's mom," I said.

"Of course!" said Mimi. "I remembered that. It will be a little weird for Casey then, right?"

I remembered talking about it with Casey before she left for camp, when she was packing up her stuff and there were clothes thrown all over her room. I knew she was not too happy to have her mom at school with her.

"I mean, I'll see her every day, all day!" she said, flopping on her bed. Then she sat up. "Oh, I'm sorry," she said. "I'll bet you'd do anything to see your mom every day."

I was quiet for a second, which I can only do with Casey. Usually I'd just quickly say, "Oh, it's okay" to get the awkward moment over.

But Casey understood. She tilted her head and waited for me to think it through.

I thought about how I'd feel if Mom was my principal. She'd always know if I got in trouble, if there was a test, if I was talking to someone or not.

"No, I get it," I said. "I mean, yes, of course I'd do anything to have my mom back. But if she was here and things were normal, I would not be too happy having her watch me all day."

Casey sighed. "That's why Gabby liked high school so much. She got rid of Mom on an hourly basis!"

"But it's not just you," I said. "Jessica Walsh's mom is a teacher there, and Jake Todd's dad is a science teacher. Claire's mom works in the lunchroom, and Richie Miller's mom works in the office. Almost every teacher or staff person there has a kid who goes through that school at some point. . . ."

"True," said Casey. "It's totally worse for Claire. I mean, her mom is probably not going to let her eat only french fries for lunch." She giggled.

"I know!" I said.

"'Claire, you come back here and get milk and some fruit!'" Casey imitated in a high voice.

"'And you sit with those nice kids over there!'" I imitated in a high voice too.

We collapsed into giggles on the floor.

"Well, thank you for showing me that someone always has it worse," said Casey.

"It is my duty as your friend to always make you feel better!" I said.

She smiled. "It's going to be a long summer without you, Miss L.!" she said.

"Don't worry," I said, laughing. "You're in for an even longer year with me when you get back."

"Ugh!" said Casey, and then she hopped up. "Okay I can only take three books, so help me decide here!"

We spent the next hour debating the books Casey had on her shelf until her mom peeked in and said, "Ladies, I can assume you're having a good time, but need I remind you that someone named Casey has to be packed and ready to go in the morning? The very early morning?"

Then we got down to business, with me calling out the things that were on Casey's packing list and

Casey folding them up and stuffing them into a giant duffel bag.

That day seemed like a long time ago now, especially with the first day of school right around the corner. Maybe everyone was right. Maybe middle school would be different. Maybe everyone was worried about it for different reasons. Maybe I should be worried about it.

On the car ride home I looked out the window at the lights of the city as they disappeared behind us. As much as I loved the city tonight, I was glad to be going home, where Sky and Nans and Grandpa were waiting for us and where I knew tomorrow morning I'd have a text from Casey.

Chapter Seven
Middle School Musings

Sure enough, the next morning there was a text from Casey, asking me what time I would be home from work. I texted her back, put on my Donut Dreams shirt, and went downstairs, where Nans and Mimi were already having coffee.

"Ready for work?" asked Nans, putting a plate of scrambled eggs in front of me. "Mimi is going to wait until Prince Sky wakes up, so I can drive you to the Park and get some things done in the office."

"Thanks," I said.

I looked from Nans to Mimi and smiled at them as I ate. It was nice having both grandmas here at the same time.

"Okay, all done! Reporting for duty," I said,

finishing up my breakfast. Mimi reached over to clear my plate.

"I can do it," I said. I didn't want Mimi to do any extra work for me.

"Oh, you get to work, honey. I'll clean up," said Mimi.

Nans raised an eyebrow but didn't say anything.

She would always say, "I am not a waitress in my own home!" whenever one of us didn't clear our plate and scrape it off before we put it in the dishwasher.

"Should I pack a snack in case you get hungry?" asked Mimi, opening the fridge.

"Uh, Mimi," I said. "I'm going to work in a restaurant. Where there is, um, a lot of food."

She spun around. "Oh, right," she said. Then she laughed. "That would be like bringing books to a library!"

"Kind of," I said.

Mimi was not the type of person to ever sit down. After dinner Nans and Grandpa would sit and talk while they had coffee or tea. When we were at Mimi's house in Chicago for Thanksgiving, she would jump up and clear the table and start cleaning the kitchen. I never saw her sit around, really. She always had projects, as she called them, or "tidying up" around the house. There was never anything out of place at Mimi's house, so she must spend a lot of time tidying.

"Well, have a good day, Lindsay," said Mimi. "I know you'll do a great job!" She gave me a kiss, and I followed Nans out the door.

When we got into the car, I said, "Nans, Mimi tried to send food to a restaurant!"

"Well," said Nans. "She means well. She doesn't know how to help when she comes, so you can't really blame her. Plus, walking into the house is hard for her, Linds. She misses your mother so much."

"Why would she miss her more at our house than at her house?" I asked, puzzled.

"Well," said Nans. "Your mom really made that house your family's home. Her stamp is all over it, from the garden in the back to her studio, to the mural she painted in Skylar's room. It's hard to be there and not think she's going to come around the corner."

"You know she's not going to come around the corner!" I said a little loudly, and Nans glanced at me.

"Well, I think Mimi does too," she said slowly. "But maybe part of her hopes that when she comes to visit, your mom will be there, just like she used to be."

For a while I thought Mom would reappear. Every day I'd wake up and think, *Maybe that was just a nightmare*, and she would be downstairs making me French toast. But after a few months, I stopped thinking that.

"Do you think she likes coming here?" I asked.

"Your grandma? Oh, very much," said Nans. "She just loves seeing you and Skylar and spending time with you. Right after your mom died, she thought about moving here because she missed you so much."

"She did?" I asked, surprised.

"Yes," said Nans. "But she was still working then, and her life was really in Chicago. So she made a promise to herself to visit as often as she could."

Just then a car pulled out in front of us really slowly, and Nans tapped the brakes.

"Holy moly!" she said. Then she peered over the steering wheel. "Is that your cousin Lily?" she asked.

I looked at the car. "Probably," I said.

"I am going to have a serious talk with her and with Charlie," Nans said. "She can't possibly think it's okay to drive like that!"

Lily was a really bad driver. Grandpa made her

park in the back of the restaurant, away from any customers, because in the first few months after she got her license, she hit two parked cars.

She didn't drive fast and she was a really nervous driver. She said she didn't like driving near any other cars, but of course, that was often unavoidable. Usually Uncle Charlie drove with her.

Nans went on and on about Lily's driving until we got to the Park.

"Lily!" she said, rolling down the window as we pulled in. "Young lady, we are going to talk about your driving!"

Lily sighed, and I gave her a look as if to say *sorry*, but I also took it as an opportunity to hurry in.

Every morning Grandpa sits at the podium right before we open and watches everyone come to work. He knows who gets there on time and who slides in. He notices if you are trying to eat a bagel while you're setting up or if your uniform isn't clean.

"Hello, lovely Lindsay!" he boomed, and I gave him a hug before I tied my apron.

Then I got out the glass cleaner and started polishing the case, even though it was already gleaming. I saw Grandpa glance over and smile.

Kelsey came streaking in a few minutes after me. "Grandpa the Great!" she said, saluting him. "Reporting for duty!"

Grandpa smiled and gave her a wink.

Kelsey went to put her bag in a locker in the back and then came bounding back.

"Okay, I want to hear all about your trip," she said.

"I'll show you," I said, noticing that Nans and Grandpa were going over the specials for the day.

I slipped Kelsey my phone. She flipped through the pictures of the art, her eyes getting bigger and bigger.

"This is so cool, Lindsay! I can't believe you got to see all this. I'm totally asking Mom if she can take me to this place."

"It was kind of fun," I said. "Ellen, the woman who worked as a guide at the museum, showed me some really amazing things."

Kelsey nodded.

"Kelsey . . . alert!" I hissed, and she shoved the phone in a drawer.

Dad and Grandpa were headed over. "Okay, guys, we have a special order today," said Dad. "The track team ordered three dozen donuts for the first track practice of the season." He handed me a piece of paper. "Can you pack up the boxes with everything they ordered? Someone will run them over at eight."

Grandpa looked over my shoulder at the order. "Looks like we're going to need some refilling of the shelves, Jane," he called to Nans.

Nans looked over and nodded, then headed back to the kitchen. Kelsey and I smiled . . . fresh donuts out of the fryer are the most delicious thing ever. I knew I'd have to elbow her to get back to the kitchen to "pick up the refills" and snag a freshly made donut.

Everyone was setting up their stations, and by six thirty we were ready to go, with the first customers coming in at 6:31. The regular breakfast customers have been coming for years.

Mrs. Selling was walking slowly, using a cane, and Rich offered her his arm to lean on. "Mrs. Selling, can I help you to your usual table?" he asked.

Mrs. Selling smiled at him.

"Coop, your grandson is just a gem," she said to Grandpa.

Our family's last name is Cooper, but everyone calls Grandpa Coop.

"Well, he learned from the best!" Grandpa said.

"The crew is all here!" Mrs. Selling said, looking around. "You're a lucky man!"

"I am," said Grandpa. "I am!"

Then he grabbed a coffeepot to start pouring everyone's morning cup.

Grandpa knew how everyone liked their coffee: with milk, with sugar, or with nothing added. The regulars didn't even have to ask him; they just sat down and he came over with their cup and saucer.

Suddenly we heard a crash, and everyone turned around to stare. Dropping things in restaurants is always the worst, especially if it's crowded. Everyone just stops and I imagine you must feel like you want to sink into the floor.

Usually what goes down is either silverware, which makes a loud racket, or worse, a dish or glass, which shatters. If there's food on a plate, it makes a huge mess. This time it was a tray, and of course, it was Lily who had dropped it.

I love my cousin, but Lily is a bit clumsy. Uncle Charlie always jokes that to have Lily work as a waitress means ordering an extra set of dishes, because she breaks so many.

Rich and Molly rushed over to help, and I heard

Grandpa sigh as he strode over with a broom.

"Poor Lily," whispered Kelsey.

"I know," I whispered back. "So embarrassing!"

Lily is really pretty and smart. She has long, wavy dark hair and bright red lips, even without lipstick, and everyone always tells her that she looks like Snow White. Someone passing through town told her she could be a model if she wanted to, in New York. But Lily really wants to be a nurse like her mom, my aunt Sabrina.

"So what outfit are you wearing for the first day of school?" Kelsey asked.

"I don't know," I said. "I haven't really thought about it. Plus, it will still be hot."

Kelsey tilted her head. "Then can I borrow one? I want to wear something new!"

"Sure," I said. "But I just don't get dressing up for the first day. We'll probably see everyone the day before school starts. So why would you dress up the next day, just to see the same people at school?"

Kelsey paused. "Well, I don't know. I guess it's like Thanksgiving or a holiday. I mean, you see your family all the time, but for certain things you just dress up."

"Yeah," I said. "That makes sense."

Kelsey looked at her watch. "This is going to be such a long day. I almost wish school had started already!"

We packed up all the donuts for the order and stacked the boxes into bags.

"All set?" asked Dad, glancing in.

"Yep," I said. "Ready to go."

"Okay, I need someone to run these over to the high school," Dad said, looking around.

"I'll go!" said Lily.

Uncle Charlie, Dad, and Aunt Melissa all said, "No!" at the same time, and Lily stomped off, looking hurt.

"Jenna!" Uncle Charlie called. "Delivery!" He tossed her his keys. "And hide the keys from your cousin!"

Nans came out of the kitchen.

"What did you say to Lily to upset her?" she asked Uncle Charlie.

Kelsey and I saw our opening. She grinned at me and nodded, and I skittered into the kitchen to grab the fresh donuts from the rack.

Lily was sitting on a stool in the corner, her lip quivering.

"Are you okay?" I asked.

She sighed. "I don't think I am cut out for waitressing," she said, shaking her head.

Nans strode back in.

"Lily," she said, "we're going to put you up front at the host station today. Do you have your regular clothes instead of your uniform?"

"Well, I have clothes to change into for after work," said Lily, grabbing a skirt and a top out of her locker and holding them up. She showed us a pretty pink top and a black skirt.

"That'll do," said Nans. "Change and then up front you go!"

Lily didn't need to be asked twice. Rich subbed in as a waiter, and Lily managed the podium up front.

She was really friendly and so chatty that people didn't even mind waiting for a table during the lunch rush. Plus, she knew exactly where everyone liked to sit. She even helped Mr. and Mrs. Block load their son Preston into his high chair.

"He never goes in without a fight!" Mrs. Block said. "You have the magic touch!"

"There's a place at the Park for everyone," said Grandpa, giving Lily a hug on her way back to the podium. "We just needed to find the right one."

Then he spun around at me and squinted. "Lindsay Cooper, you have powdered sugar on your nose, young lady!"

I looked at Kelsey, and she started laughing. "You got caught, Linds!"

"Eating the profits!" said Grandpa, pretending to yell. He acted as if he was mad at us, but he was just kidding.

※ ※ ※ ※ ※

Dad dropped me off at Casey's house after my shift ended. We had a few days left before school started. Casey's mom was at school, helping to get everything ready.

"She's in a crazed place," said Casey. "Back to school is always nuts in my house. Dad is busy too, with everyone's back-to-school visits."

Casey's dad is a doctor, and he takes care of just about everyone in town. My aunt Sabrina is a nurse in his office. She met Casey's dad when they both worked in the same hospital, and she invited him and his wife to a birthday party she was having for Uncle Charlie. That was how Casey's parents met.

Aunt Sabrina likes to say, "It's a good thing they came to my party!"

Casey led me up to her room, which is generally pretty neat, unless you open her closet or look under her bed. I looked around, and either I hadn't noticed it last week or she just put it up, but there was a picture of a boy on the bulletin board above her desk.

Usually she just had pictures of the two of us goofing around, and there were a couple cute family photos from when she was little.

But the boy photo was a new addition.

"Who's that?" I asked.

"Oh . . . ," she said. "That's my friend Matt."

"Your friend?" I asked.

"Well, I guess . . . I don't know."

"Is he your boyfriend?"

"Mom won't let me have a boyfriend yet," Casey said. "We're just pals."

I nodded, but I was a little confused as to why she had his picture up. I decided to let it go for now.

"Kelsey keeps asking me what I'm wearing on the first day of school," I said.

"Why?" Casey said. "What's the big deal?"

"Exactly!" I said, relieved.

I feel like Casey is the one person who really sees things the same way I do.

"I'll probably wear these pants," said Casey, pulling a pair out of her closet. "They're light cotton, so they'll be okay even if it's still hot out. And that top . . . now where is it . . ." She was pulling things out from under her bed. "Oh, here it is!"

It looked like a regular outfit to me.

"Do you think middle school is going to be different?" I asked.

"Well, everyone says it is," she said. "It's a different building, and we walk around to our classes and have lockers, so in that way it will be different. And we get split up into different classes, so there's that."

"But I mean, *we* won't be different, right?"

"You and me?" she asked. "Like, am I going to change overnight?"

I laughed. "No, well . . . maybe? It's just that everyone is making such a big deal about it and I think it's just . . . school starting."

"Well, I guess there's only one way to find out," said Casey.

I nodded, and we heard the front door open.

"Casey?" Mrs. Peters called upstairs.

"Up here with Lindsay!" Casey called down.

Mrs. Peters came upstairs. She looked tired.

"Well, we are set," she said. "School is ready for you. Now are you ready for school?"

Casey laughed. "No! I need more summer!"

"You know what?" said Mrs. Peters. "After today, so do I."

We followed her back downstairs and she made us a snack, just like she did when we were in first grade: sliced grapes, cheese on crackers, and what she calls banana boats, which are sliced bananas with peanut butter on top.

"Mom, how is middle school going to be different?" Casey asked, her mouth full of crackers.

"From your old school?" Mrs. Peters asked. "Well, it's a different building and a different schedule, moving around from class to class, and that takes some getting used to."

Casey looked at me. *Just as we'd thought.*

"But at this age kids are trying new things and changing, too. You might find your friends going off in new directions," Mrs. Peters said.

Casey and I thought about that for a moment.

"You mean like Brett Carr will suddenly start

playing soccer instead of being a piano genius?" I asked.

"Maybe," said Mrs. Peters. "That's why it's so exciting. You can really start figuring out who you are and what you like."

"What if we already know what we like?" asked Casey.

"Well, some kids do," said Mrs. Peters, "Brett is probably still going to be a piano genius. He's been playing since he was three. But it's always good to be open to new things too. You may not even be aware that you'd love being on the volleyball team until you try it."

I looked at Casey and giggled. She broke two fingers playing volleyball last summer, and she hates it.

"Okay, maybe volleyball is a bad example," said Mrs. Peters, laughing.

I guess I looked a little worried, because Mrs. Peters put her arm around me and said, "But whatever changes, I know you and Casey will always be friends."

"What? Of course we'll be friends always!" yelped Casey. She slid over and threw her arms around me. "Don't try on any new BFFs!"

I laughed and hugged her back. "I won't. You are stuck with me!"

Later that night, I thought about what we'd talked about. I usually fell asleep really fast, but I was tossing and turning, thinking about what Mrs. Peters had said.

What would I decide to do that was different? What if I didn't want to try anything different? I tried to stop my mind from spinning so I could get to sleep.

Finally I decided that even if middle school was different, if Casey was around, it would all be okay. Plus, I had my dreams, and I knew those would never change. The next thing I knew, it was morning.

Chapter Eight
Dress Party or Pity Party?

Mimi had talked about a "dress party" for me since she'd arrived, and even though it made me feel a little squirmy, I figured it would be fun. I don't really like being the center of attention, but I would be with my family and friends. It wasn't like I'd be strutting down a runway.

"It's party day!" Mimi trilled as she came into my room in the morning. "So much fun awaits! But first, work!"

I groaned. A day off would be nice, but the plan was for me to go to work in the morning.

Kelsey beat me to the Donut Dreams counter and was bouncing up and down, she was so excited.

"Do you think your grandma will let me keep

one of the dresses that you don't like?" she asked.

"Uhhhh," I said, unsure.

"I mean if Mom pays for it!" said Kelsey. "Oh, I'm so excited I just can't wait. Aren't you so excited to see what she picked out?"

I started to answer, but Kelsey cut me off.

"I mean, what if you hate everything?" she asked, her eyes getting wide. "That would be a disaster!"

"Well, a flood or a tornado would be a disaster," I said. "Not liking a dress is not a disaster."

Kelsey rolled her eyes at me.

"Okay, okay," she said. "But, like, everyone is going to be staring at you and expecting you to just go crazy over one of them!"

"Kelsey, no one who knows me expects me to go crazy over a dress!" I said, starting to get exasperated. "It's just a dress, and Mimi thought it would be a fun thing because—"

"Because you don't have a mom to take you shopping," Kelsey said.

I stopped stacking the napkins on the counter. "What?" I asked, a little shocked.

Kelsey looked at me. "Well, I mean, that's why we're all making a big deal about it, right? Everyone's mom takes them for their Fall Fling dress, and they thought this would kind of make up for the fact that you can't do that. We're trying to fill in for your mom."

I felt like someone had punched me in the stomach. "Um, I have to go to the ladies' room." I said, and bolted, practically running across the restaurant.

I closed the door to the stall and took a deep breath. It hadn't even crossed my mind that this wasn't a dress party—it was a *pity* party. I felt my cheeks get hot, and I could feel tears welling up in my eyes. My hands were shaking too, and I crossed my arms over my chest to kind of hold myself together.

The door to the bathroom swung open.

"Lindsay?" It was Kelsey. "I'm sorry. I'm so sorry. I think that came out wrong."

I gulped. "It's okay," I said, but my voice was shaking and the tears were starting to come.

"Lindsay, can you come out? We both left the counter, and I'm afraid Grandpa is going to notice," Kelsey said.

She waited a second and I gulped again.

"I need . . . ," I said. "I need a second, okay? Can you cover for me?"

"Of course," Kelsey said. I heard the door shut and then suddenly swing open again, and then she paused. "It's not because we feel sorry for you. It's because we want to help in case you're sad about things."

I nodded, but then realized Kelsey couldn't see me. I quickly wiped my eyes.

The door shut and I heard voices outside. A few minutes later Aunt Melissa came in.

"Lindsay?" she called. "Honey, are you okay?"

"I just have a stomachache," I said.

Aunt Melissa stood right outside the stall. "Sweetie, can you please come out?"

The bathroom door opened again and I heard Jenna and Lily whispering. Goodness, there was nowhere at the Park I could go and be alone!

Aunt Melissa tried again. "Honey, sometimes we all say that Kelsey has no filter, but in truth it affects the whole family. Sometimes things come out really awkwardly or wrong. I'd like to set the record straight."

"Is she all right?" It was Nans, squeezing in.

I sighed. "Please, please can I have a minute alone?" I sniffed. "I just . . . I just need a minute."

"The girl needs some alone time!" declared Jenna.

"Everybody out." They all filed out.

I just needed some air to think a little bit. But how was I going to walk out of the bathroom and look like everything was fine? Or leave my shift?

There was a knock on the door. Again.

"Lindsay, it's Daddy." Wow, he hadn't called himself Daddy in a long time.

"Um, this is awkward, because I can't actually come into the ladies' room, but I'd like to talk to you and not through the door."

I sighed. There was no way I could just slip back to work. I pushed open the door to the stall and looked at my puffy face in the mirror. I threw some cold water on it and patted it dry, which felt good.

When I came out of the bathroom, Nans, Jenna, Lily, and Aunt Melissa were all standing there with Dad, looking anxiously at me.

"This way," said Dad, taking my hand and leading me back through the kitchen.

He opened the back door and a breeze hit my face. Finally, I could breathe. Dad sat down and patted the step next to him. I sat there for a few minutes, just thinking. It was nice not to have to say anything.

"The thing about family," Dad finally said, "is that

they always mean well, but sometimes they don't say exactly the right things. I'm sorry you got upset."

"So are they having a dress party because they feel sorry for me?" I asked.

"No!" Dad almost yelled. "They are having a party because Mimi wants so badly to make shopping for this dress a special experience. She knows how much Mom would care about taking time to make sure you had a dress you loved, and she's trying really hard to make it a memorable thing for you."

"So why didn't Mimi just take me dress shopping?" I wailed.

Dad looked across to the trees at the end of the lot. "I think she's trying to make it a happy occasion. But in truth, it's a sad occasion for her. She feels terrible that Mom didn't get to experience this. And she feels even more terrible that you don't get to have Mom here. So her idea was to have a fun party to distract from the plain fact that everyone is missing Mom."

I was quiet for a few minutes, thinking about that. "So it's actually Mimi who feels sorry for me?"

"Well, not exactly," said Dad. "This isn't a pity party. And it's not even just about one person. It's about feeling bad that someone we love can't be here. Yes, we all feel bad about that. And we feel bad that you're missing Mom. But that's compassion. It's different from just feeling sorry for you. When you're in a family and someone is struggling or feeling bad, your family does everything they can to try to make it better. That's really what this party is about."

"Well, now I feel bad that I just made a scene," I said. "I'm really sorry."

"You didn't make a scene," said Dad. "If you want to do that, just drop a full tray at lunch like your cousin Lily."

I giggled. "Daaaad!"

"I know," said Dad. "It's not nice. And Lily is so kind, so it's especially not nice. But speaking of being nice, you should apologize to Kelsey."

"Why would I apologize to her?" I asked. "She made me feel awful!"

"She didn't mean to," said Dad. "You have to understand that no one has ever really dealt with something like this before in our family. There's no guidebook to say, 'When someone feels like this, you should do that.' People are trying and doing the best they can. Your cousin Kelsey did a lot of the organizing for the party, and she's the one who helped Mimi choose the dresses. She's been working on this for the past month. She really wants it to be a special day for you."

"She has?" I asked.

Dad nodded. "She managed to keep that a secret, which is a pretty big deal."

"Yeah," I said. "Especially in this family."

Dad laughed. "You're right. You can't hide anything in this family, that's for sure. Speaking of hiding, what do you say we get back to work before Grandpa sends out a search party for us?"

I sighed. It was nice just sitting outside.

Dad reached over and pushed my hair off my face. "You okay?"

I nodded and stood up.

When we went back inside, Nans looked up from where she was in the kitchen. I saw Dad nod to her and she nodded back. She didn't say anything, but she watched me walk to the floor. I passed Jenna, who blew me a kiss. Lily tugged on my apron bow as she passed by.

I looked at Grandpa, who was reading something at the podium. He wiggled his finger at me, and I thought he was going to give me the business for leaving the counter. Instead he gave me a giant hug.

"Remember how loved you are," he whispered. Then he went back to reading. "And now get back to work!" he said, without looking up.

Kelsey was reaching for a glazed donut when I got to the counter.

"Hi, Mrs. Lee," I said. "Kelsey is getting you a freshly made one up there!"

Kelsey held a donut, and I opened a paper bag for her to put it in before I rang it up.

"Oh, it's so nice that you girls get to work together," said Mrs. Lee.

"It really is," I said, looking at Kelsey.

Kelsey looked relieved. "Yep," she said. "Because you get to work with people who love you."

"Oh, aren't you girls just the sweetest?" Mrs. Lee said. "You are sweeter than the donuts!"

I giggled as she left. "Kelsey, we are sweeter than the donuts," I said.

"Hmm," said Kelsey. "Like, sweeter than the chocolate ones or the plain ones?"

"Oh, definitely the ones with sprinkles," I said, laughing.

"How about the crème-filled ones?" she asked.

"Yeah, those too," I said. "And absolutely the jelly-filled."

"Ugh, I hate the jelly-filled," Kelsey said. After a minute she asked, "So you aren't mad at me?"

"I'm not mad," I said.

I didn't want Kelsey to feel bad, but I guess she did, because she took out the garbage without even bargaining with me. She also wiped under the tables and chairs. We closed up the counter a little early to get ready for the dress party, and I was waiting for Dad to take me home when Casey appeared.

"Hey, what are you doing here?" I asked.

"Your chariot awaits, madam," said Casey. "We're taking you home." She waved to Jenna and Lily, who appeared with big bags of stuff.

"What's all that?" I asked.

"We are your glam squad," said Jenna. "I'm doing hair, Lily's doing makeup, and Casey is doing your nails."

"Really?" I asked.

"That way," said Lily, "you can see what you'll look like when you're all done up in the dress."

Jenna twirled her keys. "Let's go. I have orders from Kelsey to stay on schedule."

I looked over at Kelsey, who was rolling up the

mat behind the counter. I ran over to her to help.

"Go!" she said, shooing me away.

I gave her a big hug. "Thank you!" I whispered into her ear.

I didn't know what else to say, but I guess it was enough, because she hugged me back and said, "This is going to be such a fun night!"

Then she pushed me toward Jenna and Lily, and Casey grabbed my hand.

"Operation Glam!" said Casey. "Reporting for duty! I hope the Glam Squad is ready, because this one is going to need a lot of work!"

"Casey!" I yelped. "That's not nice!"

She laughed. "I'm kidding, Linds. You're perfect just as you are. Now let's go, Cinderella. The ball is starting soon!"

Chapter Nine
Operation Glam!

"First, a shower," demanded Jenna when we got home. "We start from scratch here."

I wrapped myself in my bathrobe, wondering what else was ahead of me.

Mimi was downstairs setting up and had chased me out of the living room. I noticed that the dining room table was already stacked with plates and teacups. I peeked out the window and saw Dad and Nans unloading boxes of food from the car.

Dad was taking Skylar night fishing, and Sky was so excited he was running up and down the hall and nearly collided with me.

"Watch it!" I said.

He stopped. "Why are you taking a shower at the

end of the day? Are you going to bed early?"

"No," I said. "I'm getting ready to try on some fancy dresses for the Fall Fling."

Sky looked confused. "Well, I'm going fishing, so maybe Dad will let me take a bath in the river!"

"Eeeuuw," I said. "You will take a bath with a toad. That's disgusting!"

"That would be so cool!" Sky said, and ran down the stairs. "Dad! Dad! Lindsay said that maybe I can take a bath with a toad!"

"That's not . . . ," I started to yell after him, but then decided to let it go.

I took a quick shower, and washed and combed out my hair. I wrapped my towel around me and sat down on the bed.

Jenna and Lily both looked at me seriously as if they were about to perform surgery.

"Makeup first," said Lily, and she started dusting powder on my face.

"Not too much!" said Jenna. "Nans will not be happy."

Lily nodded. "She doesn't need much," she said, winking at me. "Because she's naturally pretty."

I blushed.

Then Jenna took out a blow-dryer and a curling iron and was tugging at my hair for what seemed like forever. Casey was carefully putting bright pink polish on my toenails.

I heard the door opening and closing downstairs and started to get a little nervous. "So how many people are coming?" I asked.

"Well, the four of us," said Jenna, "and Casey's mom, Aunt Sabrina, my mom, Molly and Kelsey and Nans and your grandma Mimi."

"And Gabby!" said Casey.

"Right," said Jenna. "Gabby too!"

"Twelve of us?" I yelped.

"Yeah, it takes at least a dozen people to decide on one dress," said Lily, smirking.

Finally they all stepped away, looking at me. Lily reached over and pulled some hair behind one of my ears. Then she nodded at Jenna.

"Okay, go look," said Jenna.

I went over to the mirror. At first it didn't even look like me. Well, it looked like me, but more glamorous. My hair was shiny and wavy and it didn't even look like I had makeup on, just a little pink on my cheeks and lips.

I grinned. "I think I'm ready for my big modeling job!" I tossed my hair and struck a pose.

"We're coming down!" Jenna yelled down the stairs. I heard everybody cheer and applaud.

"We're ready!" Kelsey yelled back up.

Lily helped me into a button-up shirt so I wouldn't mess up my hair, and I pulled on a pair of jean shorts.

I followed Jenna, Lily, and Casey but stopped as I got halfway down the stairs.

The living room was set up like a giant dressing room. The sofa and chairs were pushed along the wall and someone had rolled up the rug. There was a rolling rack like you see in a big store, and it was filled with dresses. Next to the rack was a line of shoes, some of which I recognized as Kelsey's. A full-length mirror was propped up on the wall, and I saw Nans's sewing basket next to it.

There were balloons tied to the chairs, and flowers in bunches on the end tables.It definitely looked like a party.

"Well, come on down, Ms. Lindsay!" said Mimi. "Let the dress games begin!"

I stood next to Mimi, not sure what to do.

"Okay," said Kelsey. "Here are all the selections."

She pointed to the rack. "You decide where you want to start. Then you try on all the dresses until we find the perfect one."

Everyone was looking at me and I felt a little shy.

Mimi pulled out a green dress. "I thought this would be so pretty," she said. She grabbed my hand. "But come look and pick one to start."

I took the one Mimi was holding. "This is nice," I said. It was dark green with light green ruffles on the skirt.

"Okay, that's the first one then!" said Kelsey. She pointed to the corner of the room, where someone had hung a bedsheet. "That is your dressing room!"

"And I am your official dresser!" said Molly. "Some of these dresses have a lot of buttons!"

I giggled and followed Molly to the corner and behind the sheet.

I pulled on the dress and Molly zipped it up. "It fits!" she yelled out.

"Good job on getting the sizing right!" Nans said to Mimi.

"Oh, I'm so glad," Mimi replied.

I looked at Molly. "Well, you have to come out of the dressing room so everyone can see!" she hissed at me.

I took a deep breath and shuffled out, and then Molly pushed me into the center of the room.

"Oh, you are just so lovely," sighed Mimi.

"That's beautiful, Lindsay," said Aunt Melissa.

"I love that color," said Mrs. Peters.

"You look like grass," said Skylar from the hall.

"Sky!" Nans scolded, and everyone started laughing.

"Okay, we're on our way out now and just came to say goodbye," said Dad, pulling Skylar. "Gone fishing! Lindsay, you look beautiful as always, but choose the dress that makes you happiest, okay?"

"And one that doesn't look like a soccer field!" called Skylar.

Everyone cracked up again, and Dad scooted Skylar out the back door.

"Well," I said. "Now all I see is grass."

"No grass dresses!" said Kelsey. "Next!"

Casey tugged at a purple dress. "This is nice!"

"Okay," I said, grabbing it.

Molly helped me get out of the soccer dress and into the purple one, which was a lot more complicated. It had a halter top that tied behind my neck and a zip on the side that was really tricky to pull up. Then there was a light purple sash that tied around the waist.

"What's taking so long?" demanded Kelsey.

"I'm going as fast as I can," Molly yelled back.

"Girls!" said Aunt Melissa.

Molly stood back and scrunched up her nose. "I don't love it," she said. "But go see for yourself."

The skirt swished when I walked out. I wasn't sure what to do, so I stood next to Mimi.

"Well, that's pretty too," she said. Then she steered me to the mirror.

The dress reminded me of something, but I couldn't put my finger on it.

Casey came over and put her hand on her hip, looking at me. "Uh, do you remember that doll you had that you used to tote around everywhere?"

I looked at her blankly.

"Cressida!" said Mrs. Peters.

"Cressida!" said Nans. "Oh my, I remember Cressida!"

"Yes!" I squealed. "She was my favorite doll. She came in a big poufy purple dress . . . oh." I peered in the mirror. "I look like Cressida!"

"You totally do!" laughed Casey.

We both collapsed into giggles.

"Next!" said Kelsey.

Mimi handed me a pink dress while Molly tugged the Cressida dress off me. The pink dress had a long pleated skirt and the body was really fitted. It had buttons that ran up the side.

When Molly was finished fastening the last in the long row of buttons, she tilted her head to the side. "This one has possibilities," she said.

I walked out and over to the mirror.

"Ohhhh," said Mimi. "Oh, that's so pretty. And I love the color."

Nans and Aunt Melissa nodded.

"Try these with it," said Aunt Sabrina, handing me a pair of silver sandals.

Nans, Mimi, Aunt Melissa, and Aunt Sabrina were all smiling, but Kelsey put her hands on her hips.

"It's really pretty," she said. "I love it. But somehow it just doesn't seem like *you*."

"Oh but I like it!" said Casey.

"I feel like there's something missing," said Kelsey.

"Um, guys, I'm right here," I said.

"Yes," said Mimi. "Let's ask Lindsay what she thinks. Lindsay?"

"I like it," I said, watching myself in the mirror. "It's really pretty."

"Well, there are a lot of others," said Kelsey, pointing toward the rack. "You should buy something you love, not something you like."

I looked at the rack, and one dress caught my eye. "Well, I may as well try on a few more," I said.

I toted the one I chose into the dressing room. "Molly!" I called.

"I need a break!" said Molly. "I'm getting a snack! There's food set up in the dining room, people!"

Everyone laughed, and I heard people moving around to the dining room.

At first I felt a little hurt that everyone had abandoned me for some food, but then I thought, *Well, when I put this one on, I can make a grand entrance.*

Chapter Ten
True Blue

I pulled the next dress on myself and easily zipped it up. It felt light and flowy, like I could run around in it if I wanted to. I turned around to leave and I heard a gentle *swish, swish* from the bottom of the skirt, which made me happy for some reason. I felt like I had on a magical fairy dress, like I could float across the room without my feet touching the floor.

Everyone was in the dining room when I came out, so I walked over to the mirror to get a look before anyone else could see.

I stopped when I got close. There was a picture of Mom that we had on a table in the front hall. She was in a cornflower-blue dress, smiling at the camera, her head tilted back and her eyes crinkled up with laughter. It was taken when Mom and Dad were at a fancy party in Chicago, right before we found out Mom was sick.

I looked down and realized the dress I was wearing was the same purplish-blue color of her dress. It made my hair look darker and my lips look brighter. I looked a lot like Mom in that picture.

"Oh!" I heard a gasp behind me. It was Mimi, and her hand flew to her mouth.

Everyone rushed back into the living room and everyone, it seemed at once, said, "Ohhhhh!"

"That's it!" said Kelsey. "That's the magic dress!"

"Oh, Lindsay," said Mimi. "You look so beautiful."

I spun around. "I look like Mom."

Mimi looked startled. Then she smiled. "You do. You look exactly like her, and that color . . ."

"It's her favorite color," I said, remembering. "True blue."

"True blue," Mimi whispered, and I could see her eyes were filling up with tears.

The room was really quiet. Mimi came over and put her hand on my shoulder, looking at me in the mirror. I didn't know if she was looking at me or if she was seeing Mom.

True blue was a color Mom made up. She always said her favorite shade of blue was a little purple, a little white, and a little gray mixed together. She mixed it up on her paint palette and even kept some in a paint jar on her shelf. It was hard to find anywhere, but this dress was the closest to her shade of true blue I had ever seen outside of her paintings.

And suddenly, I missed her more than ever. My grandmothers were here and my aunts and cousins and BFF, but the one person who was missing was Mom, and I really, really wished she were here. I missed her all the time, but at this moment, wearing this dress, it hit me hard that she wasn't here. I started to cry, and I just couldn't stop.

Mimi hugged me tight, then Kelsey and Nans, and Aunt Melissa and Casey. There were so many arms around me that I didn't know whose hands or arms belonged to who. Soon we were a big pile of crying arms.

Finally it was Molly who yelled, "And break!"

We were all so startled we laughed. Casey handed out tissues, and everyone blew their noses.

Mimi cupped her hand under my chin. "You okay?" she asked.

I nodded and smiled. "Mom would want me to wear this dress," I said. "It would make her so happy."

Tears streamed down Mimi's face, but she was smiling. "She would have picked this out herself," she said. "It's the perfect dress for you."

Nans knelt down next to me. "Someone hand me my sewing box."

Jenna passed it to her and Nans started pinning the dress up a little. Lily helped me put on a pair of sparkly sandals, and Jenna pulled my hair so it was half up, half down. I still looked like me, but with a dreamy dress.

"Done!" said Kelsey, satisfied.

Everyone clapped.

"Whoo-hoo Team Dress!" said Molly.

"And now we eat donuts!" said Casey.

Nans and Mimi helped me out of the dress and I slipped back into shorts and a shirt. I followed Nans into the kitchen to help with the donuts.

"Do you know why I love donuts, Lindsay?" she asked.

"Because they're delicious?" I answered, watching her roll out the big ball of dough.

"Well, yes," she said. "But see how I make them?

You use the dough cutter to cut out circles from the rolled-out dough."

I nodded as I watched her. I had seen her make donuts millions of times. She could probably make them in her sleep.

"Each donut is a circle," she said. "You drop the circles in the oil or the fryer and scoop them right out when they're done."

I watched as she tossed the circles of dough into bubbling-hot oil in the pan.

"The thing is," said Nans, "they have a hole in the middle, but they're surrounded by dough." We both watched as the dough bubbled.

"That hole," she began, "reminds me that sometimes there's a hole inside us. Sometimes it gets filled or sometimes we don't notice it as much, but it's always there."

She scooped out the puffed-up donuts with a slotted spoon and laid them on paper towels to drain.

"But there's always dough surrounding the hole." She put down the spoon. "Do you know what I'm trying to say?"

"Sort of," I said. "We all have a hole in us?"

Nans cocked her head. "Sometimes we do.

Sometimes those holes close up and sometimes they get smaller, but they're always there. But no matter what, those holes are surrounded."

"So our family is a donut?" I asked.

Nans laughed. "Kind of. I like to think the donut is more of a symbol of our family. That even when there are holes that can never be filled, there's a lot of sweetness totally surrounding them to help them not get any bigger."

She looked at me like she wanted me to say something, but I wasn't sure what.

"Lindsay," she said, putting her hands on my shoulders and looking into my eyes. "You are surrounded by people who love you. I want you to always remember that."

I smiled. "I will."

"Hey, where are those donuts?" Molly yelled as she stormed into the kitchen.

Nans laughed. "Right here! Right here!"

I helped her pile them on a platter, and Molly carried them out to the table.

When I sat down in the living room, I couldn't help noticing Kelsey sneaking looks at a certain silvery gray dress. She kept walking by it and touching it.

"Why don't you try that on?" I asked.

She spun around. "Me? Oh, I couldn't. These are all for you to try on."

"Well, I already have my dress," I said.

"But it's your party," she said.

"If it's my party, then you have to do as I say," I teased.

"Well," she said, looking longingly at the dress. "This is really beautiful."

"Come on," I said, and pulled her toward the dressing room.

I helped put on the silver dress. It had lots of layers that made it shimmer when Kelsey moved. There were these see-through ruffles that went around the bodice and short sleeves that kind of looked like wings. I stood back.

"Kelsey, you look like a fairy princess," I said.

"Like for Halloween?" she asked.

"No, no, like a beautiful princess," I said. "Go look!" I pushed her out toward the mirror.

"Hey!" said Molly. "Kelsey, those dresses are for Lindsay!"

"Well, I already found mine," I said.

"So the rest are up for grabs?" asked Molly.

"Girls, girls!" said Aunt Melissa. "These were chosen for Lindsay. This is her party. We will find your dresses later!"

"Well, if they like some of these, why not let them try them on?" asked Mimi. "We have so many. Plus, it will save me the trouble of returning all of them!"

Aunt Melissa looked at me. "Are you okay with this? These dresses were for *you* to choose from."

I nodded my head. "I made Kelsey try this one on. She loves it, and look how pretty she is in it!"

Everyone gathered around Kelsey. "It is beautiful on her," said Mimi.

"Well," said Aunt Melissa. "If you don't mind me just buying this from you, then we'll have two girls with dresses for the Fling."

"Two down!" cried Mimi. "And two to go. Casey and Molly, do you see anything you want to try?"

Casey looked at her mom.

"Go ahead," Mrs. Peters said. "If the dress store comes to you, why go to the dress store?"

Casey took the pink dress off the rack. "I know you didn't love this," she said. "But I do. Can I try it?"

I grabbed her hand and pulled her toward the dressing room. "We'll be right out!"

The dress had looked nice on me, but it looked amazing on Casey. Casey's mom pulled it up a little and smoothed down the skirt.

"Oh, I love that on you!" said Mrs. Peters.

"All right, Molly," I said. "Do you see anything you like?"

Molly smiled. "Well, I kind of like the soccer-field dress," she said.

We all started laughing. "So try it on!" said Mimi. "Don't let Sky be your fashion police!"

Molly came out in the dress. She stopped, did a spin, and put her hand on her hip.

"Dahling, I think this might be just fabulous!" she said, and we all laughed.

"You know, it really suits you," said Aunt Melissa, smiling.

"Let me fix your hair," said Jenna, pulling Molly's hair up off her neck.

The green dress looked nothing like a soccer field on Molly; it looked perfect.

"You all need to put on your dresses so we can take a picture!" said Lily.

So we all scrambled into our dresses as Nans scolded us to watch out for all the pins she'd put in them. I was in a blue dress, Casey in pink, Kelsey in silver, and Molly in green.

"It's a rainbow of pretty!" said Aunt Sabrina. "Get in close so I can fit the whole dress into the shot!"

We stood together, arms around each other, smiling.

"Everyone say, 'Fall Fling'!" said Aunt Sabrina.

"Fall Fling!" we all yelled, and held still for about a second.

"Dance party!" cried Jenna, and she put on some music.

We were dancing around while Nans and Mimi shouted at us to be careful with the dresses. But we didn't care. We all grabbed hands and danced, laughing and twirling.

Chapter Eleven
Post-Party Chat

Later that night, my dress was hanging on the back of my door and I could see the outline of it in the dark as I pulled up the covers in bed.

Sky had thrown a fit about going to sleep, and through the wall I could hear Dad reading to him to try to soothe him, even though it was late.

I wasn't supposed to have my phone in my room at night, but I had actually forgotten to leave it downstairs in the charging station, and I was too tired to go back down anyway. I grabbed it and flipped through the pictures Aunt Sabrina sent us from the party. We all looked happy and goofy, and I had to say those dresses looked pretty good on us.

My favorite picture showed me in the middle,

smiling and sort of spinning, with everyone around me in a circle, laughing.

I looked hard at that shot. I realized as I scrolled through that both my grandmothers were there, both my aunts, my BFF, and all my girl cousins. There was one person who was missing, of course, and that was Mom.

Dad knocked on my door. "From what I heard, it was a pretty good party," he whispered, coming in.

By the time Sky and Dad came home, the party had wrapped up and all the dresses had been packed up.

"Dad," I said, then stopped.

"Yes, honey?"

"I missed Mom tonight."

Dad sat on my bed. "I did too," he said. "But I heard your dress was her favorite color." He squinted at it in the dark.

"It's true blue," I said, smiling.

"Sometimes," said Dad, "I'm reminded of Mom in ways that make me feel like she's still here."

"Like a ghost?" I said, alarmed.

"No, no," Dad said. "Like in the way Sky laughs exactly like her, or the way your dress for the dance ended up being her favorite color."

"Nans says that we're like donuts," I blurted out.

"Hmm," said Dad.

"She says that we have holes in us, and I guess for me that hole is where I miss Mom."

"Oh, I see," said Dad.

"But that like a donut's shape, we're surrounded by people, in a tight circle, so that hole doesn't get any bigger."

"That's exactly right," said Dad. "You have so many people who love you. They may drive you nuts, but they love you. And you might not like that they surround you all the time, but they always have your best interests at heart."

I laid back on the pillow and yawned. Suddenly I felt really tired.

"Okay, young lady, it's time for bed." Dad reached over to switch off my night-table light when I noticed a little bouquet of flowers next to my stack of books.

"Hey!" I said, sitting back up.

There were violets and bluebells in a little vase.

"Oh," said Dad. "Sky found those today when we were fishing. We weren't sure where to put them when we brought them home, and Mimi thought maybe you would like them."

I smiled. "They remind me of Mom," I said.

"They do," said Dad, smiling back. "True blue."

"She's still here, sort of," I said, yawning.

"She's always with us," said Dad quietly.

I flopped back onto my pillow. I couldn't keep my eyes open. I knew Dad was still sitting on my bed like he did when I was younger, waiting for me to fall asleep, but I was so tired I couldn't even say good night.

It was nice having him there, and knowing that Sky was asleep on the other side of the wall. Mimi and Nans and Grandpa were all in the house, all of us together, one big circle.

I pulled my blanket tighter, and as my eyelids fluttered, all I saw were shades of blue.

Chapter Twelve
A New Beginning

And just like that, before I knew it, it was the first day of middle school. It was still pretty warm, so I just put on a short-sleeved purple T-shirt that Mimi had bought for me, a silver bangle bracelet, and a new pair of jeans. I wanted to look nice and fresh, but I didn't want to get super dressed up or make too big a deal out of it.

"Well, don't you look beautiful!" Nans said, as I sat down at the kitchen table.

She plopped down a plate of homemade pancakes (my favorite) in front of me, and I saw she had made a smiley face with syrup.

I laughed. "Thanks, Nans," I said as I dug into the pancakes.

She was still staring at me. "Yes," she said, nodding approvingly. "You look perfect. Lovely, but not overly done."

I smiled at her. "That's just what I was going for," I told her.

Then I added, "You remembered Mom used to make pancakes on the first day of school." Nans nodded.

"And she would always say the same thing to me," I said. "She used to tell me to have a great day, and to remember to always be my 'own special self.' It felt a little silly when she kept saying it as I got older, but by then it was sort of like a first-day-of-school tradition, and she had to say it. I made her say it."

I smiled at the memory, but then I was startled to look up and see Nans's eyes filling with tears.

Oh no! That was the last thing I wanted.

Luckily, just at that moment, Skylar came bounding into the kitchen.

"Oh boy, pancakes!" he yelled. "Awesome!"

Nans dried her eyes and put a plate in front of him. She tried to lighten the subject.

"What did your mom say to Skylar on the first day of school?" she asked.

I grinned. "Keep your mouth closed when you eat."
Nans laughed.

☀ ☀ ☀ ☀ ☀

When I walked through the doors of Bellgrove Middle School, I paused in front of the mural that my mom's students had made in her honor.

I had been worried that seeing it every day would make me sad, but I actually felt really happy when I saw it.

I noticed that some students had painted in bright, cheery colors, and others had sketched in charcoal. Parts of the mural showed wildflowers in bloom (which my mom would have loved), and another section showed a stormy sky, and then another section showed a rainbow.

Each student painted whatever they wanted and didn't worry about whether it blended in with the rest of the mural. The end result showed so many different personalities and styles that it was all the more beautiful.

I reached out and ran my hand gently across the colors. "Always be your own special self," I whispered. "Thanks, Mom."

Hole in the Middle

In that moment I could feel her presence. Even though I couldn't see her anymore, I knew she was always with me. And I would always have my family and friends to help me through rough times, and make the hole inside me a little smaller.

I took a deep breath and walked into my first class.

Still Hungry?
Here's a taste of the second book in the

series, **So Jelly!**

Chapter One
I Don't Like Change

My friend Sophia was looking at me like I was crazy. "But you have a job!" she said. "That's so cool!"

I sighed and pushed my bangs off my face. They were really starting to annoy me, and I had to decide if I should just let them grow out or get them trimmed.

"Well, yes and no," I said. "Yes because it's cool to work at Donut Dreams, but no because it's hard work, and I'd rather be doing a lot of other things, like going out for pizza tomorrow with you."

I work at my family's restaurant, the Park View Table, after school Fridays and one day on the weekends. This week I'm working on Sunday.

Inside the Park there's a donut counter, Donut Dreams, that my grandmother started with her homemade donuts, which are kind of legendary around here. I work at the Donut Dreams counter with my cousin Lindsay.

I don't mind working with my family, but it's hard when my free time is eaten up by work while my friends get to hang out and do things—like how Sophia, Michelle, and Riley were planning to go out for pizza after school the next day.

"Hey! Are you coming with us tomorrow?" asked Riley as she plunked herself down at the lunch table.

"She's working," said Sophia with her mouth full.

"What?" said Riley, and then without waiting for an answer, she called out, "Oh hey, Isabella, over here!" Sophia and I looked up to see Isabella walking toward us.

Sophia, Michelle, Riley, and I have been what my dad calls "four peas in a pod" since we were toddlers. We have other friends too, but everyone knows we've always been a crew. But when school started, Riley was suddenly really into hanging out with Isabella, who seems to be joining us at lunch on the regular.

Whenever I complain about having more people around instead of it just being the four of us, my mom always replies, "When it comes to friends, additions are always okay, but subtractions are not."

So I'm trying to be okay with more friends, but sometimes I'd like to subtract Isabella and just make it Sophia, Michelle, Riley, and me, like it always has been.

Sophia wrinkled her brow a little bit when Isabella sat next to Riley. No one else noticed, but if you've known her for eleven years like I have, you'd have noticed.

Michelle uses a wheelchair, and she wheeled her way over to my side. "Scootch over," she said, and I made room for her.

"Hey, Isabella," Sophia said.

Isabella put her tray down and looked like she was going to cry.

"What's wrong?" Sophia asked.

"You guys, I totally think I am going to fail my coding class," Isabella said. "I just do not get it."

"Bella, it's only the second month of school!" said Riley. "You'll get the hang of it." I had never really heard anyone call Isabella "Bella" before.

"Yeah, chill out, Isabella," Michelle said. "Take a deep breath. It's going to be fine."

"Ugh," said Isabella. "It's just so hard and there's so much pressure. I mean, they all say that everything starts to matter in middle school if you want to go to college!" she complained.

"You still have a long way until college!" I said. "No need to worry about it now. Trust me, my sister Jenna is in high school. That's when the pressure really starts."

That wasn't entirely accurate. Jenna had been talking about college for a good seven years. Jenna is the oldest of my siblings (she's a junior in high school) and a little bossy. Actually she's *a lot* bossy.

She and Lindsay, and even my adopted sister Molly, who is a few months older than me, are always talking about going away to college. My parents are okay with this, but I can tell they don't want us to go too far. Jenna talks about how she wants to go to a school in California, which kind of scares me.

She is also always talking about "getting away" from our small town, like it's some bad place to be. She loves reading about big cities or seeing movies that take place in big cities. One year for her birthday, Jenna asked for a bunch of travel guidebooks to all the big cities in the world, even though she's only been to one of them: Chicago.

I don't understand why you'd ever want to leave Bellgrove. This town is home to me. I mean, sure, it would be nice to go somewhere sometimes without being totally recognized, but then again, seeing familiar people is kind of nice.

I like that the person who cuts my hair has been cutting it since I was a baby; that the librarian, Ms. Castro, has known me since even before I could read; and that every year we do the same things, like go apple picking at Green Hills Orchards in September before we get the same hot apple cider at Corner Stop. I like living within a few minutes of just about every single person in my extended family. All those things to me are not just dull things we're stuck with—they're traditions and familiar people and they make me feel safe.

I know I'll have to go to college in another town because there isn't a college here, but the closest state university, where my mom and dad and aunt and uncle went to school, is about two hours away. Mom keeps reassuring me that I can come home on the weekends if I want to.

When we have these conversations, Jenna just rolls her eyes and says, "Really, Kelsey? Stretch yourself! Open your eyes to new adventures! It's only two hours away!"

But to be honest, two hours away from *everything* I know sounds like plenty of an adventure for me.

"So," Sophia said, jolting me back to the table. "Are you going to try out for the field hockey team like we talked about?"

I nodded. "Yeah, it sounds fun, and Mom really wants me to do something active," I said.

Mom and Dad are always taking us on walks or bike rides, even when it's freezing cold outside. I wasn't too sure how I'd like playing competitively, but I love to be outside, especially in fall when the air turns crisp and smells so good.

"As long as I can still keep my hours working at the restaurant," I added.

"But your grandparents own the place where you work!" Riley said. "I'm guessing they can work with your schedule!"

"You'd think," I said, "but Grandpa is a stickler for

not giving us special consideration. We still have to clock in a certain amount of hours, unless our grades slip. School comes first."

"So if you fail a few tests, you can get out of work," snorted Isabella, or *Bella*.

"If I fail a few tests, I'd have a lot more to deal with than missing work," I retorted, kind of snapping at her. I don't know why, but Isabella gets under my skin sometimes.

"Well . . . ," said Riley. She paused, and Sophia and I looked up. "Bella and I were thinking about doing soccer instead of field hockey."

I caught Sophia's eyes, which looked as surprised as mine.

"That's great!" Michelle said. "So now I'll take photos of the soccer team as well as field hockey." Michelle takes awesome photos and dreams of being a professional photographer someday.

Riley bit her lip. "The thing is, I'm not sure I'm great at field hockey, and I know I'm a pretty good soccer player, so I want to try out for the team."

Isabella looked at her and smiled. I had a weird feeling they'd talked about this before. Sophia looked at me.

I shrugged. "Well, you should always do what makes you happy," I said. "Soph and I will be a team of two on the field hockey team."

Riley looked at me strangely. "Okay," she said. "I just don't want you guys to be disappointed that we all wouldn't be playing field hockey together. But you're right, you have each other on the field."

"Yep, we have each other," said Sophia.

It was quiet for a second, and then Michelle asked me, "So how is work going?"

I shrugged. "It's okay. A lot of the time I'd rather be somewhere else, but everyone in the family works there, so it's my turn to step up. Or at least that's what Grandpa said."

"Do you get to eat the extra donuts?" asked Isabella. "Because oh my goodness, I could eat, like, a dozen of those at a time."

"No," I said. "We donate the ones that haven't sold at the end of the day."

Sophia and I exchanged a smile, because everyone always asks me that question.

People think if you work at a donut shop you eat donuts all day, every day. In elementary school, Joshua Victor asked me if our house was made of donuts.

"Well, you've been known to show up with donuts," teased Riley, and I laughed.

I do try to bring donuts to my friends' houses when we have extra or when Mom brings them home.

"Work perk!" I said.

"Oh, I can almost taste those cider donuts," moaned Isabella. "Shoot, now all I want is a cider donut. It's definitely better than . . . whatever this lunch they're serving is."

"My favorites are the coffee-cake donuts," Michelle said. "And the chocolate ones with rainbow sprinkles. Or the plain glazed ones. Or . . . "

"We get it. You like donuts!" Riley said with a laugh.

Just then the bell rang. We gathered up our stuff and hustled out to our next class.

As we were going into the hall, Sophia grabbed my arm and hissed, "What is going on?"

I sighed and shrugged. "She is really good at soccer," I said.

"Well, Riley may be good at soccer, but she'd better be good at being our friend," said Sophia, and before I could respond, she shot off down the hall.

Isabella, Riley, and Michelle turned in a different direction, heading toward language arts, where they were in a class with my sister Molly. Before they went into their class, I caught Molly's eye as she walked by in the hallway.

It was obvious she could tell something was up. She was looking at me as if to say, *What's going on?*

But I just said, "You'd better catch up to your potential new soccer teammates," and hurried off to my own class.

Middle school was different, that's for sure, and I don't think I like change.

Chapter 2
Sisterly Love

My dad is usually home after school. He teaches woodshop at the high school during the year, and in the summer he works for a construction company that his brother owns.

Molly and I dumped our stuff in the cubbies that he built us, kind of like lockers, near the back door and found him in the kitchen, making a snack.

You'd think that because Mom's family owns a restaurant she'd be a really good cook, but she totally is not. She jokes that's why she married Dad, because he can whip up anything and it's always delicious.

I sniffed. "Ooh, popcorn!"

"And hello to you too, honey," said Dad.

He was popping kernels in a deep pot on the

stove, and the kitchen smelled like a movie theater. He pushed a plate of sliced bananas and peanut butter toward us.

"Dad, where are the raisins on top?" Molly asked.

Dad used to call this snack "ants on a log," which we thought was hysterical. He slices the bananas lengthwise, smears on peanut butter, then scatters raisins on top. He used to tell us that they were ants crawling on a banana log. We thought it was funny, but it could also explain why I hate raisins . . . I mean, eww, eating ants! I always pick them off.

"We're out," said Dad. "It's still back-to-school season, and Mom and I have been so crazed and busy we haven't been able to get to the market."

"So, ant-less?" asked Molly.

"Yes, I'm afraid we are out of ants, Molls," said Dad. "So I am making it up to you with some popcorn."

"If we put these on top . . . ," said Molly, cocking her head and thinking.

"They could be clouds on a log," I said, taking a piece of hot popcorn.

"They could be fluffy sheep on a log," said Molly. "That makes more sense. Why would clouds be on a log?"

Dad grabbed the grocery list that Mom kept on the fridge door and wrote *raisins* on it.

"Okay, I'm still finishing up this summer job and I have to install the cabinets I built," he said. "So I'm going to head out until dinnertime."

This year Mom and Dad have been letting us stay in the house without them home, but only during the day. Dad is always here after school, though, which is nice, even if he's sometimes really annoying and asks a ton of questions about our day.

Today, though, Dad was in a hurry.

"Okay, dinner is in the slow cooker," he said, "so whatever you do, do not turn that thing off, or we'll all starve. Mom will be home by five thirty. We both have our phones at the ready, so just text or call if you need anything."

"Where's Jenna?" I asked.

"At work," said Dad. "Wait, is she at work? This new schedule . . . ," he muttered.

He scurried over to the bulletin board in the kitchen, where Mom keeps a monthly calendar and writes down who goes where on each day. Dad calls it the Command Center.

"Yep, yep, she went to work after she had a

student council meeting, and Mom will bring her home when her shift ends," said Dad.

"Dad, did you just lose track of a daughter?" teased Molly.

"No!" said Dad, but we all laughed.

Mom is crazy detail-oriented. Everything at home is organized beyond belief. Like the cans in our kitchen cabinets are basically alphabetized. Her socks are folded a certain way and arranged by color.

Maybe it's because she's an accountant, and, as she says, accountants have to be precise about things because they work with numbers. As the accountant for the restaurant, she makes sure that all the finances are up to date, like the staff gets paid, the bills are paid on time, and at the end of the month the restaurant isn't spending more money than it's making.

Uncle Charlie does all the ordering, everything from napkins to food to supplies like extra water glasses, because in a restaurant you are always breaking glasses. Uncle Mike runs Donut Dreams, where I work. Nans plans out the menus and figures out the daily specials, and makes her special donuts, and Grandpa . . . well, as Grandpa proudly tells everyone, he steers the ship and keeps it on course.

Everyone has their "own lane" as they all like to say, and they say that a lot to each other, as in "Hey, get out of my lane!" when they step on each other's toes. Everyone has a different role, but we all work together.

Dad builds things, so he has to be precise too, but in a really different way. When he's building something, he's all about measuring, and remeasuring, and cutting things accurately so everything fits together. But when he isn't building something he isn't too precise, which drives Mom crazy.

Once he went to pick me up at dance class . . . only I wasn't at dance class, I was waiting for him to pick me up at the library. He also once dropped off Molly for a playdate at the wrong house.

He's always messing up the laundry, too. Just last week Jenna was struggling and trying to get into a pair of jeans until she realized that they were mine; Dad had put them away in her closet instead.

"I have it together!" said Dad, a little indignantly.

"Okay," said Molly. "So you know you have to take me to soccer, right?"

"What?" said Dad, looking panicked.

"Practice starts at six," said Molly. "It's on the board!"

Dad went over to the bulletin board. "Oh . . . yeah, there it is."

Just then our phones lit up with a text message from Mom.

> **All good? Everyone home?**

"It's like she senses when we need her," said Molly, laughing.

"She probably just wants to check in to see how school was," said Dad.

He texted back,

> **All OK.**

Molly added,

> **Dad forgot soccer.**

About two seconds later, Mom called Dad's phone.

He picked up immediately and reassured her that everything was fine and that he would be home in time to get Molly to soccer, and that he would take me with him if she wasn't home from work yet. He then left the house to finish his work, and the house was nice and quiet.

Not that my older sister Jenna or Dad or Mom are loud people, but you notice when they are around. I can always hear Mom puttering around the house, or Jenna playing music. Sometimes I even hear Molly practicing with her soccer ball against a wall somewhere, stopping only when Mom or Dad yells, "Molly, cut it out!"

I wondered if our house would still be like this once Jenna left for college, when it would just be the four of us. It seems so weird that she wouldn't be here every day. The thing about having two sisters is that you get really used to having them around.

"Do you ever wonder what it will be like when Jenna moves out?" I asked Molly, who was sitting right next to me at the counter.

She looked up from her phone. "What?" she asked.

"When Jenna goes to college," I said. "When it's just the four of us instead of five, do you worry that it will be weird?"

Molly wrinkled her forehead. "I dunno," she said. "Like will we miss her?"

"Well, we'll miss her, sure," I said. "But I mean,

what will dinner be like without her? What will the weekends be like?"

"Well, the weekends will be easier, because we don't have to worry about making noise and waking her up," said Molly, in her very matter-of-fact Molly way.

This was true. Jenna liked to sleep in on the weekends, and she was always barking at us to keep it down. Molly and I are early risers.

"But won't it be like one person is just missing?" I asked.

I knew Molly wasn't always into these kinds of conversations, so I was pushing it.

"Things change, Kelsey," Molly said in a tone that sounded like she was explaining it to a two-year-old.

"Oh, never mind," I said, and pushed away my chair. Molly was making me feel worse instead of better.

Sometimes getting people to talk in our family was impossible. My cousin Lindsay was the one I used to talk to about everything. We're just about the same age and grew up together, so in a lot of ways we are more like sisters than cousins.

But Lindsay's mom, my aunt Amy, died a couple years ago after being sick for a long time. If you talk to

Lindsay, she doesn't burst into tears or anything, or at least not usually, but I'm always really careful when I talk to her now, especially if I'm talking about my family.

If, say, I complain about Mom, I'm worried that Lindsay is really thinking, *Oh, well, at least you still have your mom.* If I tried to talk to her about how weird it would be with Jenna gone, I'm afraid she would think, *Well, she's just going to college. She's coming back. But my mom isn't.*

Lindsay is actually really sweet, so I don't think she'd think those things on purpose, and she would never say them to me out loud, but there are things I just can't talk to her about anymore.

"You'd better get your homework started before Mom gets home," said Molly.

I looked over, annoyed, and I noticed that while I'd been sitting there thinking, she had already set up her laptop and was typing away.

Molly is only eight months older than I am, but she acts like she is my much older sister. So between her and Jenna, I really feel ganged up on sometimes and like I am the baby of the family.

Jenna and Molly are a lot alike. They are both super organized and they belong to a million different clubs and are always thinking about their next project or what they'll be doing in ten years.

Dad calls me Kelsey Dreamer because I guess I daydream a lot, and I like to take my time doing things. I just don't feel that crazy rushing sense or the competitiveness that Jenna and Molly seem to have been born with.

I opened my laptop, logged in, and clicked over to the homework page and sighed. Ugh. There is *so* much homework in middle school.

There was no way I'd finish before dinner, which I hated. I liked to be able to relax after dinner, and have what Dad calls downtime, when you kind of just do nothing.

I peeked over at Molly. "Do we have to read this whole chapter for history?" I asked.

"Yes," said Molly, her hands flying over the keyboard.

I opened the window and breathed in.

"Ooh, someone is burning leaves," I said. I love that smell.

I positioned my chair so the breeze from outside tickled my face. It was a shame to spend such a beautiful afternoon inside doing homework.

Then I looked over at Molly again. "Did you finish reading it already?" I asked.

"Yeeesss," said Molly with a hint of annoyance, not looking up from her laptop.

"What is it about?" I asked.

"KELSEY!" Molly screamed so loud I jumped. "You have to do your own homework! I'm not going to do it for you!"

"I wasn't asking you to do my homework," I said crossly. "I was just curious."

"If you're curious, then open the book," said Molly, and she sounded exactly like Mom when she said it.

I sat there for a few more minutes, listening to the leaves crinkle in the wind. Dad was going to make us help rake them up on the weekend.

"Kelsey, I can help you if you get stuck, but you have to start and you have to try," said Molly.

"Okay," I said, eating some more popcorn. "This tastes so much better when Dad makes it on the stove than in the microwave," I said. "And it's fluffier."

Molly looked at me sideways. "Thanks for the review, Princess Popcorn," she said.

I snickered.

Molly looked over and giggled too. Then she

grabbed a handful and chewed. "You're right," she said. "This does taste good."

She glanced over at me with a mischievous twinkle in her eye that I know well and said, "Sheep on a log! Well, what if those sheep *flew*?"

Then she hurled a fistful of popcorn at me.

"MOLLY!" I screamed, shaking popcorn from my hair but laughing.

I tossed some down the back of her shirt.

"Oh, it is *on*, Princess Popcorn!" she said, and showered me with half of what was in the bowl.

We were both throwing the popcorn and cracking up when we heard my mom say, loudly, "Girls, what on earth is going on in here?"

Jenna peered around her. "Are you maniacs having a popcorn fight?"

We both said, "No!" while popcorn fell from our hair, and we tried not to giggle.

Mom sighed and handed me the broom and Molly the dustpan. "I don't even want to know. And I don't want to see anything either . . . please clean up this mess."

I started sweeping and Molly scooped up the piles, but we couldn't stop laughing.

"Sheep on a log!" Molly whispered, trying to stifle her laughter.

"What are sheep on a log?" asked Jenna.

"What happens when you don't have ants," I said, and Molly started to laugh even harder.

"What?" asked Jenna, but she started to laugh too.

Sometimes that happens when we're all together. We just start laughing and we can't stop, sometimes over something silly and sometimes over nothing at all.

Mom looked at the three of us cackling and threw up her hands. "I don't get it," she said. "But the sound of you three girls laughing is always the best."

Molly and I settled down and cleaned up and Jenna started to set the table. I felt another surge—this was so nice—the three of us together with our own secret kind of language.

Why would you ever want to leave it? I just wished it could stay this way forever.